CHEERLEADERS

GOING STRONG

CHEERLEADERS

CHEERLEADERS #24

GOING STRONG

CAROL ELLIS

SCHOLASTIC INC.
New York Toronto London Auckland Sydney

ISBN 0-590-40341-9

12 11 10 9 8 7 6 5 4 3 2 1   12   6 7 8 9/8 0 1/9

Printed in the U.S.A.   01

CHAPTER

It was December fourteenth, and Tarenton looked like the picture on a Christmas card. Six inches of newly fallen snow blanketed the ground, the sun was dazzling in a winter-blue sky, and everywhere people were on the move — to the shopping malls, the skating rinks, the ski slopes, and the Christmas tree lots.

It was perfect holiday weather, but Olivia Evans couldn't enjoy it. For one thing, she was inside the Tarenton High gym, where it had to be at least eighty degrees, she thought. Not that she minded being in the gym, warming up for the cheerleading practice. Olivia was captain of the Varsity Squad, a group of six cheerleaders who dazzled the crowds with their complex, dynamic routines, and she loved it. She even loved the warm-up exercises. While she put her body through a series of leg stretches, walkovers, and sit-ups, she could let her mind wander, usually to something completely unrelated to cheerleading. Sometimes she thought about homework, trying to solve a tricky math problem or come up with a spectacular subject for a research paper. Other times she thought about clothes or just let her favorite rock song play over and over in her head.

Today, though, Olivia was thinking about David Douglas Duffy. Which was the second reason she couldn't enjoy Tarenton's winter wonderland. If she weren't in the gym, she'd be outside, but not skiing or ice-skating or sledding. She'd be rushing from store to store, totally ignoring the gorgeous weather, trying to find the perfect Christmas present to give to David.

It had to be special, because David Duffy was special. Olivia had met him two months before, and after a shaky start, the two of them seemed to be heading toward a romance, the first one Olivia had had since her old boyfriend, Walt Manners, had moved away. A year older than Olivia, David was a freshman at the junior college, wrote a weekly sports column for the local paper, and made Olivia's heart beat a little faster every time she saw him.

As she started in on some wide leg stretches, Olivia pictured David in her mind. Tall and slender, he had a bouncy, springy walk, full of energy and enthusiasm. His face was alive, its single dimple flashing whenever he smiled, his

2

lake-blue eyes twinkling whenever anything amused him, which was pretty often. His sense of humor was quirky and offbeat, just like his hats. David loved hats, and probably had one for every day of the week, Olivia thought — a soft blue yachting cap, a tweed racing hat, even an ancient leather one that he claimed was worn by a World War I flying ace. Now that Olivia thought about it, she couldn't remember ever seeing David without some kind of hat in his hand or on top of his thick blond hair.

Sitting on the gym floor, Olivia tugged up her yellow legwarmers and grinned. A hat would be the perfect gift. But what kind of hat? It couldn't be anything ordinary; it would have to be something different, funky, something to match his sense of humor and make his eyes light up with a laugh.

Olivia glanced around the gym and spotted Jessica Bennett, whose green eyes squinted with concentration as she did a series of slow back walkovers. Olivia couldn't help noticing that Jessica did them perfectly, but for once, she didn't feel jealous. It had taken a long time, but she was finally beginning to accept the fact that Jessica was as good a gymnast as she was, that she deserved to share the spotlight with Olivia. It hadn't been easy — Olivia was ambitious, talented, and used to being the star of the squad, the one who made everyone "ooh" and "ah" when she hurtled her small lean body through the air in some daring gymnastic move.

3

But Jessica was ambitious, too, and just as talented. She wasn't looking to outshine Olivia though; all she wanted was to be the best she could, and Olivia understood that. That's the way she was, too. Besides, Jessica was friendly, smart, and totally committed to the squad. What more could a captain want? Advice, Olivia thought wryly, advice about what kind of hat to buy David for Christmas. And Jessica might be just the right person to ask. She was comfortable around boys, and she seemed to understand them, maybe because she had two older brothers.

Olivia scooted across the floor and waited while Jessica finished her exercise. "That looked great," she told her.

Jessica tossed her long brown hair out of her face and smiled. "Thanks, Olivia. I just hope I look as good during the game Saturday night."

"Don't worry," Olivia said, "you'll be fine. But listen, I need a favor."

"A favor?"

"Well, just some advice, really. About David." Olivia ran her fingers through her shining brown hair. "See, I want to get him a hat for Christmas."

"That's a great idea," Jessica said with a grin. "I couldn't help noticing that he has the best collection on the block."

"That's the problem," Olivia told her. "I mean, I can't just get him any old hat. It's got to be different, special. And," she went on, "I thought maybe you might have some ideas. Or maybe your brothers would know. Maybe there's some kind of hat that's popular in college. Something David would get a kick out of."

"I'm not sure," Jessica admitted. "I think the last time Gary and John wore hats was when they were in grade school, but I'll ask them. And I'll think about it, too."

"Great. Thanks, Jessica." Olivia checked the clock and jumped up. "I guess I'd better do some more exercises before the coach comes and asks me why I haven't worked up a sweat!"

As Olivia cartwheeled across the gym floor, Jessica laughed and went back to her own warm-up exercises. She was pleased that Olivia had asked her advice. It meant that they weren't rivals anymore, or at least that they were friendly rivals. But as she watched the squad captain's incredibly limber body turn itself into a human pinwheel, Jessica couldn't help feeling jealous. Not because Olivia was so talented, but because Olivia was so obviously happy with David Duffy.

It must be nice, Jessica thought with a sigh, to just jump right into love like it was the deep end of a swimming pool and not be afraid of getting in over your head. Of course, once you were in, it was either sink or swim, and that was a chance Jessica wasn't about to take, not even with Patrick Henley.

The minute she thought of Patrick, Jessica immediately felt like squirming. She wasn't ready to fall in love, she'd made that very clear. Love

5

didn't last. Patrick had been in love with Mary Ellen Kirkwood for three years, and that hadn't lasted. Jessica's father had died when she was ten, so that hadn't lasted. Love was a risky business as far as Jessica was concerned, and she wasn't ready for it. If only Patrick would back off and give her some breathing space, then things would be fine.

Of course, she had to admit, she didn't want Patrick to back too far off. He was bright, and funny, and good-looking, and she liked him better than any boy she'd ever met. And he wasn't *really* pushing her that hard, either. But he was getting impatient, she could feel it every time they were together. He wanted to know where he stood with her, and she could hardly blame him for that. She wasn't being fair. She should tell him to find somebody else, somebody who wasn't afraid to jump headfirst into love. But that wasn't what she wanted, either.

Jessica sighed again, then stood up and touched her toes. Forget Patrick Henley for now, she ordered herself. Think about something else. Hats, for example. A hat for David Duffy. That's a nice, safe subject.

When she saw Olivia bounding back across the gym, Jessica called out, "How about a cowboy hat?"

Olivia stopped, poised on the balls of her feet, and closed her eyes. "I'm trying to picture it," she said. "I don't know if David's the ten-gallon type."

6

"You're getting David a hat?" Tara Armstrong asked.

"I'm thinking about it," Olivia said. "Got any ideas?"

Tara tilted her head to one side, her silky red hair tumbling around her face. "A cowboy hat's a possibility," she agreed. "Or maybe . . . I know! How about one of those long, long stocking caps? Striped in some really outrageous colors?"

"Come on, Tara," Sean Dubrow chimed in. "The guy's not a clown."

"No, but he doesn't take himself too seriously either," Tara shot back. "Being able to laugh at yourself is a very appealing quality."

Sean grinned until his dark eyes sparkled, and Tara found herself grinning back. Sean might not be able to laugh at himself, but other than that, he was extremely appealing. Too bad he knew it, Tara thought.

But even though Sean was as full of himself as just about any boy she knew, Tara couldn't help wanting to be with him. His dark hair and eyes, fabulous build, and cocky personality were like magnets that kept pulling her closer. The trick was not to let him know how she felt, which was why Tara had spent the entire warm-up period trying to decide whether to go to all the holiday parties with him, or to turn down a few of his invitations, just to keep him guessing.

"Well, then," she said to Sean, "if you don't like my idea, what kind of hat would you suggest?"

Sean stopped in the middle of a sit-up and pretended to think about it. Actually, he didn't give two beans about what kind of hat Olivia got for Duffy. If Olivia was hooked up with David, then she wasn't available for Sean, and Sean was only interested in available girls. Girls like Tara Armstrong.

Of course, he couldn't let Tara know what he thought. Dealing with girls like Tara was like being in a card game — you had to play your hand close to your vest, or you'd lose. And Sean had no intention of losing. That's why he'd decided to cohost a Christmas party with Lisa Hutton. It was exactly the sort of move that would keep Tara on her toes.

Putting on his best poker-face, Sean shifted his glance from Tara to Olivia. "I vote for something sexy," he said.

Olivia frowned. "Like what?"

Sean turned his face in profile and ran a hand over his hair. "Like the bare-headed look," he said with a wink.

Olivia laughed. "Well, I've got three opinions," she said. "A cowboy hat, a stocking hat, and no hat at all. Does anyone else have an idea?"

"I don't know *what* you should buy," Hope Chang said, pushing her shining dark hair behind her ears, "but I do know where you should buy it."

"Where?"

"At Langston's."

"Langston's is nice," Tara said, thinking of Tarenton's largest department store. "But why are you pushing it, Hope?"

Hope sat up a little straighter. "Because I'll be working there," she announced. "As soon as Christmas break starts."

"You're kidding!" Tara burst out. "What do you want to do that for?"

"Well, it's the holiday season," Hope said, "and I have lots of presents to buy."

"That's ridiculous," Tara told her. "Your father's a doctor. You can't be hurting for money. Besides, I thought you'd spend the vacation studying."

"Right," Sean teased. "Didn't you tell me you got a B in social studies last quarter? Better look out, Hope, your grade point average might sink below four-point-oh."

"I thought you'd dust off your violin and play it all day," Olivia said. "You told me last week you really needed to practice."

"Well, I do," Hope admitted with a laugh. "But the job's only part-time, so I'll still be able to do other things." Even though she laughed, Hope felt uncomfortable. She didn't mind the teasing, but she wasn't crazy about the image her squadmates had of her: quiet Hope, always studying, always practicing, always doing the right thing. Hope wasn't looking to switch personalities, but she did want to fit in more, to be more like other people. And most other people she knew didn't hole up in their rooms with books and violins. It was almost Christmas vacation, and everybody would be out, going to parties, working to earn extra money for presents, having fun. Hope wanted to be out there with them.

"Is that really what you want to do, Hope?" Peter Rayman asked. He was looking at her curiously, as if he'd just read her mind and didn't believe what she was thinking. Normally, Hope would have been pleased. Shy, lanky Peter Rayman was the first boyfriend she'd ever had, and it was a wonderful feeling to be on the same wavelength with him. But she was touchy about this job and she didn't want anyone, even Peter, to know the real reason she'd taken it.

"Sure it is," she told Peter, not looking him in the eye. "And remember, everybody," she said to the rest of the squad, "I get an employee discount, so. . . ."

"So I'm going to buy every one of my gifts at Langston's," Tara announced.

"You'll have to wait your turn," Sean said. "I just remembered this fabulous sweater I saw in the window there. I figured it was out of my price range, but now that we've got someone working on the inside, I think I'll check it out again."

"You'd better look out, Hope," Jessica warned. "You'll have to work overtime just to keep up with all the extra orders."

"I hate to say it," Olivia put in, "but if Mrs. Engborg catches us goofing off, *we're* going to be filling orders — for extra workouts."

"Does that mean what I think it means?" Sean asked.

"Afraid so," Olivia laughed. "Let's get back to the warm-ups."

"Slave driver," Sean grumbled, but he said it with a grin and immediately started in on some deep knee bends.

As they all went back to work, Olivia felt like laughing out loud. At the beginning of the year, she wouldn't have bet more than a dime that this group of six different people could ever turn into a team. Part of it had been her fault, she knew it. She'd missed the old squad so much that she was always comparing them, which hardly helped morale. But the rest of them had had their problems, too. Sean and Tara tended to be lazy; they'd wanted the glory without the work. Jessica was so single-minded about being good that she came across as a snob at first. Peter had let Sean intimidate him, and that kept him from doing his best. And Hope, who was much more talented than she thought she was, had been so paralyzed by feelings of inferiority that she'd goofed on some of the simplest routines.

Now, though, they were finally coming together, Olivia could feel it. They could joke together, they could tease each other, they could relax with each other. And it was showing in their routines. Their coach, Ardith Engborg, was giving them harder ones to perform now, and they tackled them like Olympic contestants going for the gold. Olivia couldn't wait for Saturday

11

night's game. It was the last one before Christmas break, and they had a new routine that was going to bring the fans to their feet.

We'll knock their socks off, Olivia thought happily. Then she glanced at the big clock on the gym wall and frowned. Mrs. Engborg was twenty minutes late, which was completely out of character. Usually the coach was early, tapping her foot impatiently as she scrutinized every move they made.

Just as Olivia was wondering whether she should go searching for Ardith, she heard the coach's voice through the open gym doors.

"Do I have to say it again?" Mrs. Engborg asked in a tone of complete exasperation. "My answer is no. Now, I don't want to discuss it anymore."

The coach's voice was loud enough to make the six cheerleaders stop in midexercise and look toward the door. As they watched, Mrs. Engborg appeared, accompanied by a slender, dark-haired man who looked to be about thirty. He said something no one could hear, but which obviously didn't sit well with the coach, who shook her blonde head vehemently.

"Who is that man?" Tara wondered out loud. "He looks awfully familiar."

Sean chuckled. "He should. His picture's in the paper at least once a week. His name's Judson Abbott," he went on, "and he's got his finger in just about every political pie in Tarenton — the

12

town council, the school board, you name it."

"He sounds ambitious," Jessica commented.

"He's cute," Tara remarked.

"I get the feeling the coach isn't too impressed with him, though," Peter said. "Look at her."

Peter was right. Ardith Engborg looked angrier than any of them could ever remember seeing her. Her lips were clamped together in a thin line and her eyes were blazing.

"Judson Abbott better watch out," Sean said. "I wouldn't be surprised if the coach hauled off and punched him."

No one was even pretending to do any exercises now; they were completely caught up in the scene between their coach and Judson Abbott. There was obviously some kind of battle going on, and even though they knew Mrs. Engborg would never punch anyone, they didn't doubt for a minute that the feisty coach would emerge the winner.

Out in the hall, Judson Abbott leaned close to Mrs. Engborg and spoke very quietly. The six cheerleaders strained their ears, but no one could hear a word he said. Then, a strange thing happened. Instead of getting angrier, which the squad fully expected her to do, Ardith Engborg backed away a few steps, stared at the floor for a long time, and then, finally, she nodded.

Judson Abbott gave her a satisfied smile and went on talking, but the coach, who kept her eyes on the floor, didn't seem to be listening.

"I'd give anything to know what that's all about," Tara whispered tensely.

"Whatever it is, it's not good news for the coach," Sean said. "She looks like somebody just slipped a noose around her neck."

CHAPTER

"You're on top,
And you know it!
We're right with you,
So let's show it!"

Hands on hips, shoulders back, the six Tarenton High cheerleaders faced the hometown crowd. Their distinctive red and white uniforms looked like they'd been chosen with Christmas in mind, and the smiles on their faces reflected the holiday spirit that gripped the whole school. It was Saturday night, it was the final game before Christmas break, and best of all, with a score of 72–40, the Tarenton Wolves were annihilating the Deep River Killers.

With a lift of her chin, Olivia set the squad in

motion. Short skirts whirling, the four girls peeled away from Peter and Sean in a series of perfectly executed cartwheels. The two boys gave a simultaneous clap of their hands and then sprang backwards, heels over heads, in side-by-side back flips. With Tara and Hope now twirling their pompons in intricate patterns of flashing color, Jessica and Olivia began simultaneous hand-springs from opposite ends of the line. The hand-springs brought them back to the center, where Sean and Peter stood poised to lift them up to their shoulders.

It was a new routine, and each time they'd practiced it, something had gone wrong. This time, everything had gone right. There'd been no false steps, no missed cues, no one out of place. It had gone exactly the way it was supposed to, and it looked exactly the way it should — a complex, dynamic routine charged with energy and performed with perfection.

> "Tarenton's a winner,
> We know it!
> We're behind them,
> So let's show it!
> Yea, Tarenton!"

As Olivia and Jessica leaped lightly to the floor, the crowd roared its approval, stamping their feet and clapping rhythmically.

Faces flushed with excitement as well as exertion, the six cheerleaders gathered at the bench, while the Wolves and the Cougars took the floor again.

"Were we incredible, or were we incredible?" Sean wiped his face with a towel and gave the rest of the squad a cocky smile.

Olivia smoothed back her hair and laughed. "Should we take a vote?"

"What for?" Tara asked, sipping from a cup of water. "It'd be unanimous, right?"

"Wrong," Peter said. He tried to sound serious, but his grin gave him away. "We weren't just incredible; we were *absolutely* incredible!"

"I'll vote for that," Sean said, laughing. "And if that routine didn't put a smile on Mrs. Engborg's face, then the lady's got lead in her jaws."

They all glanced toward the lower bleacher where their coach was sitting. It had been obvious to everyone since Wednesday's practice that something was bothering Mrs. Engborg. She'd been Ardith the Grouch, as Sean privately dubbed her — quiet if practice went well, and ready to jump down their throats at the slightest mistake. It was completely out of character. Ardith Engborg was always fair with them, as long as they gave their best. And they'd given their best all week, so they knew they couldn't be the problem.

Tara had tried to convince the rest of them that it was just the season. "My mother always gets extremely touchy during the holidays," she'd said. "All the parties and shopping and stuff — she says she's ready to collapse just thinking about everything she has to do."

But now, as the squad looked at Mrs. Engborg, it was obvious that more was troubling her than just the pressure of the holidays. Chin in hand, their small, blonde-haired coach was gazing vacantly at the gym floor. She wasn't frowning, but she wasn't smiling, either, and she seemed completely oblivious to everything that was going on around her.

The squad issued a collective sigh. "Can you believe it?" Tara complained. "It's like she doesn't even know we're here. I mean, we just gave our best performance ever, and I don't think she saw a single bit of it!"

"I know," Olivia agreed, "but there's nothing we can do about it now. Come on, let's do the 'Slam-Dunk Cheer.' "

In a flash, the six cheerleaders were back on the sidelines. Stamping their feet and clapping their hands in unison, they soon had the crowd on its feet, chanting along as the clock wound down and the Tarenton Wolves raced to the opposite court for another basket.

> "Slam! Dunk!
> What's that sound?
> It's the Tarenton Wolves,
> The hottest team around!
> Go, Wolves!"

Forty-five minutes after the game was over, Ardith Engborg, still sitting on the same bleacher, watched her Varsity Squad file back into the

18

gym. They'd all showered and changed; they looked relaxed, refreshed, and extremely pleased with themselves.

They have every right to be pleased, she thought, feeling a surge of pride as she looked at their shining faces. They weren't just coming along anymore; they'd arrived. Tonight, they were as good as any squad she'd ever coached, and if this were a perfect world, they'd only get better.

But it wasn't a perfect world, she reminded herself. You try to play an honest game, but sometimes the deck is stacked.

As if to push that unpleasant thought out of her mind, Mrs. Engborg gave a brisk shake of her head and stood up.

"Okay," she said to the squad, "I know you're all starving for pizza, so I won't keep you long. I have two things I want to talk to you about, and the first one is the practice schedule for vacation."

The cheerleaders exchanged knowing glances. They'd been expecting this, so they weren't surprised.

"We'll practice every day except Christmas Eve and Christmas, New Year's Eve and New Year's Day, and Sundays," Mrs. Engborg announced, passing out copies of the practice schedule. "That may sound like a lot, but it'll be worth it. You'll still be in shape when the break's over, so you won't find yourselves having to play catch-up."

The coach paused and gave them one of her rare grins. "Not that I'd be too worried about your

19

catching up," she said. "After watching you tonight, I'd be willing to bet you could tackle any routine I threw at you."

"Great!" Sean said exuberantly, as the rest of the cheerleaders basked in the praise. "Go ahead, Coach, throw one at us. We're ready!"

"Now? Are you crazy?" Tara laughed, punching him playfully on the shoulder. "I refuse to move another muscle until I get something in my stomach. I'm absolutely famished!"

"I know what Sean means, though," Hope said to the coach. "Thanks, Mrs. Engborg. It really helps a lot to know you have confidence in us."

"Right," Peter agreed. "For a while there, we weren't even sure you'd seen us at all."

"Oh, I saw you," Mrs. Engborg assured them. "And I was proud of you." She let them relish her words for a few more seconds, and then, clearing her throat, she went on. "Now, for the second thing I want to tell you," she said, and most of the cheerleaders noticed that her grin had completely disappeared. "Starting at Monday's practice, this squad is being expanded. By one person."

A stunned silence greeted this announcement, and Mrs. Engborg took advantage of it. "Most of you probably know him," she went on quickly. "He's a senior here at Tarenton, and his name is Robinson Ladd. Beginning Monday, he'll be our seventh Varsity Cheerleader."

* * *

"I don't believe it!" Olivia said for what seemed like the hundredth time. She brought a slice of pepperoni pizza halfway to her mouth and then stopped, shaking her head in amazement. "Just like that, boom! She decides to put somebody else on the squad."

The six cheerleaders, along with David Duffy and Patrick Henley, had come to The Pizza Palace expecting to celebrate Tarenton's win, the squad's fantastic performance, and the beginning of Christmas vacation. Instead, the eight of them were hunched over one of the small tables, discussing Ardith Engborg's bombshell and trying to recover from the fallout.

"And she wouldn't tell you why?" David asked.

Olivia, still in shock, just shook her head again, but Sean had no trouble finding words. "Are you kidding? She wouldn't give us the time of day. All she'd say was, 'That's the way it is. Period.' The lady was definitely not communicating."

Jessica leaned forward to put her elbows on the table, and the movement caused Patrick's hand to slide off her shoulder. Jessica hadn't planned for that to happen, but in a way, she was relieved that it had. Patrick, with his dark hair and sparkling eyes, was powerfully attractive. It was much safer to keep some distance between them, no matter how little.

"What bothers me," Jessica said now, "is what it's going to do to our routines. The six of us are finally a team. Adding a seventh person is going to be like . . . like. . . ."

"Like having two left feet," Peter finished glumly. "What I want to know," he said, remembering how hard he'd worked to make the squad, "is how Rob Ladd managed to become a cheerleader without having to try out."

"He did try out," Hope said. "I remember. He didn't even make the first cut. But maybe . . . I don't know, maybe he's gotten better."

"I don't care if he's turned into a champion gymnast," Sean declared. "The guy doesn't belong with us."

"Just who is Rob Ladd, anyway?" Patrick asked.

"My question exactly," David said with a grin. "But wait, let me get my notebook out. This'll make a great story."

"Not for us, it won't," Olivia told him. "You aren't really going to take notes, are you?" David loved his job, and Olivia knew he worked hard at it, but she wished he wouldn't actually start writing down everything they said.

As if sensing her feelings, David stuffed his small spiral notebook back in his pocket and took her hand. "Okay," he said cheerfully, "I'll take mental notes. How's that?"

"Mental notes will be fine," Olivia said, squeezing his hand.

"Good." Leaning back in the booth, David pushed his battered yachting cap to the back of his head and stared around the table. "So? Who's Rob Ladd?"

"His full name's Robinson Ladd," Sean said with distaste. "His father's a state senator."

"I don't really know Rob," Jessica said, "but I've seen him in the halls a lot. He's always got at least two girls following him around like puppy dogs."

"That's because he's gorgeous," Tara blurted out.

The other five cheerleaders stared at her as if she were talking about a rattlesnake.

"Well, he is!" Tara claimed, feeling flustered. Actually, she was slightly intrigued with the idea of Rob Ladd being on the squad. He was definitely good-looking, with sandy hair and a tall, slender build. He walked as if he expected people to make way for him, and Tara had wanted to know him ever since she first set eyes on him. Now was her chance.

One look at the others, though, and she decided she'd better keep that information to herself. "All I said was that he's handsome," she protested, pushing her red hair back from her face and reaching for her Coke. "And that's a purely objective observation."

Everyone hooted, but even though Sean joined in the laughter, he wasn't really amused. He knew Tara, and when she said Rob Ladd was gorgeous, that meant she was interested. And that's what was bothering Sean, not that he'd ever admit it to anyone. Robinson Ladd, with his lean, sculpted face and his upscale wardrobe, was a magnet for girls. As Jessica said, at least two of them traipsed around after him wherever he went. And now that he was on the squad, he was going to have an even bigger female following. Rob Ladd was competition, and Sean didn't like it at all.

"You guys aren't giving me anything," David complained good-naturedly. "So far, all I've got are his name, who his father is, and that he's gorgeous. What kind of story is that?"

"A rotten one," Olivia said. Then, in spite of her outrage, she yawned widely.

The yawn was catching. Suddenly everyone was tired of discussing the situation. What was the point? Mrs. Engborg had spoken, and Mrs. Engborg's word was law, even if it was unfair.

Only David, ever the reporter, was unwilling to drop the subject. Slipping an arm around Olivia's shoulder as they all got up to go, he said, "There's a story here somewhere. I can smell it. And I'm going to follow my nose until I get to the bottom of it."

CHAPTER

Patrick watched as Olivia and David, and Hope and Peter crossed The Pizza Palace parking lot, heading for their cars. Both couples were holding hands, he noticed, which seemed like a natural thing to do when you were crazy about someone. He glanced at Jessica, who looked great with her brown hair spilling out from under a green wool cap, and decided to join the crowd. Reaching for her hand, he drew her a little closer to his side and smiled. "I'll tell you what I'm thinking about if you'll tell me what you're thinking about. Deal?"

Jessica laughed softly. "Deal. You go first."

"Okay." Patrick gripped her hand a little more tightly. "I was thinking about all the great times we're going to have now that vacation's here." Opening the door of his van, he waited while

Jessica climbed in, then went around and got in the driver's seat. "There're a couple of parties coming up, both of which I'm asking you to, and . . . let's see, do you like to ice-skate?"

"I love it," Jessica said.

"Good, so we can do that. And how about this?" he suggested. "I pick you up nice and early one morning, and we drive to this place in the hills where you can chop your own Christmas tree. And after we do that, we drive back with the two best-looking trees around and then we stuff ourselves at the Pancake House. How does that sound?"

Jessica thought about it for so long that Patrick was afraid she might have something against live Christmas trees. "It's a tree farm," he explained. "Trees have to be thinned out anyway, to make room for the young ones. It's not like we'd be destroying a forest or anything."

"I wasn't worried about that," Jessica said, laughing again. "And I don't want you to think I'm lazy, but I don't know if I'm much of a chopper."

"You think *I* am?" Patrick asked, grinning. "I just figured that between the two of us, we could get the job done. Besides, we're not talking about gigantic trees here."

"You're right," she agreed, and was silent again.

"So?" Patrick asked after a moment. "What do you think? Does that sound like fun?"

"Oh, sure, Patrick," Jessica said slowly, "it

sounds great." I *want* to go, she thought. Why can't I relax and say yes?

Patrick sighed, started the van, and drove it out of the parking lot. He'd just mentioned a bunch of things they could do during vacation, and he knew they weren't earthshakingly exciting, but still, they were fun, especially when you did them with someone you cared about. But the way Jessica was acting, he felt like he'd suggested they get flu shots together. What was the matter with her, anyway?

Slow down, Henley, he told himself. Maybe something *is* the matter. After all, she's here with you, right? She wouldn't be riding in your van, talking about chopping down Christmas trees, if she couldn't stand your company. Right? Right.

"Hey, Jessica," he said as casually as possible, "you seem kind of down. Everything okay?"

Jessica turned from the window and sat up a little straighter. Some actress you are, she told herself. Patrick's all excited about his plans for vacation, and you sound about as enthusiastic as a sleepwalker. Did you really think he wouldn't notice?

Fingering the zipper on her puffy orange jacket, Jessica stole a quick glance at Patrick. He was concentrating on the road, which had patches of ice, and he was frowning. You're responsible for that frown, she thought guiltily. Sometimes you let him believe that you care about him in a romantic way, and then you pull the rug halfway out from under him by acting like a zombie. Why

27

don't you just go ahead and pull the rug all the way out? What are you afraid of — that you won't have a date for any of the holiday parties, if you tell him the truth?

Jessica knew that wasn't the answer. Without being conceited, she knew she could easily have plenty of dates. They'd be the right kinds, too — friendly, casual dates with all the emotional weight of a handshake.

There was already more than a handshake between her and Patrick, and even though she was afraid to take it any further, Jessica wasn't ready to put the brakes on it, either. And if she just stopped worrying about the whole thing, at least while she was with Patrick, then maybe things could go on at a nice, steady pace.

Catching Patrick's eye, Jessica stopped fiddling with her jacket zipper and smiled. "We made a deal," she said, "and I know I was supposed to wait until you were finished, but I can't stop thinking about Rob Ladd." That was partly true. She *was* wondering why Mrs. Engborg had decided to disrupt the squad now that things were going so smoothly.

"It just doesn't make any sense," she went on. "Even if Rob turns out to be fantastic, we'll still have to change all our routines, and that's going to take a lot longer than Christmas break. When vacation's over, we'll look like we did in September. That's going backward, if you ask me. It doesn't make sense," she said again.

"It's weird, all right," Patrick agreed. Talking

about a cheerleading crisis wasn't exactly romantic, in his book, but at least Jessica didn't look bored out of her mind anymore. He had a sneaking suspicion that Rob Ladd wasn't the only thing bothering her, but since he didn't know what else was, he figured it was better not to push it. Why ruin things?

Patrick glanced over at Jessica and smiled. She sure is beautiful, he thought. Then as he looked in the rearview mirror and saw Peter Rayman's car turn down Hope Chang's street, his smile disappeared. He wasn't the jealous type, but right at that moment, he couldn't help envying Peter. At least the guy knew where he stood with Hope. And Patrick, who drove his own garbage truck and co-owned a moving business, would have bet a week's wages that Peter wasn't having to listen to nonstop talk about the latest development in the Varsity Squad.

Patrick would have lost his bet. Peter *was* pretty sure about Hope's feelings for him, but as he drove his green Ford toward the Changs' house, he was completely confused about everything else.

For one thing, Hope hadn't stopped talking since they'd left The Pizza Palace. Not that Peter minded. He liked everything about Hope, including the sound of her voice. But nonstop talking just wasn't her style.

Plus, she was talking about Rob Ladd. Which was normal, Peter knew, considering how surprised they'd all been at Mrs. Engborg's announcement. But there had to be other things on Hope's mind. Her new job, for one. Why wasn't she talking about that? Especially since he'd tried to ask her about it at least fifteen times.

"So," Hope said, as Peter pulled the car to a stop, "I guess we'll just have to make the best of it. What do you think?"

Peter turned the engine off and stretched his arm along the back of the seat. "I don't know," he said, his fingers touching the shoulder of Hope's red wool jacket, "but since we don't have much time before you have to go in, I think we should drop the subject." Smiling, he kissed her softly on her cheek, then her mouth, and finally rested his lips against her glossy hair.

"You're right." Hope laughed, shifting slightly so she could lean back in the circle of his arms. "This is much nicer than talking about Rob Ladd."

They were quiet for a moment, and then Peter said, "Hope? I'm really curious about something."

Your job, Hope thought silently.

"Your job," Peter said aloud. "I mean, I think it's great if that's really what you want to do. But somehow, I just can't picture you working in a department store, especially during the holidays. It's going to be total chaos, and you don't like chaos."

Hope frowned and leaned forward slightly. This was exactly what she'd been expecting, which was why she'd monopolized the conversa-

30

tion all the way home. Tomorrow was her first day at work, and she was nervous enough about it without having to defend herself. "Peter," she said quietly, "I'm sure I can handle chaos as well as anyone else. Besides, I think it's going to be fun. I'm looking forward to it."

"You are?" he asked in surprise.

Hope shook her head. "Now you sound like my parents."

"I do?" Peter was even more surprised. Being compared to Dr. and Mrs. Chang was the last thing he expected. The three of them didn't have much in common, except that they all cared about Hope. At first, the Changs hadn't even wanted Hope to date Peter, because he wasn't Asian. Finally, after Hope told them she was going to do it anyway, they'd accepted it, but Peter knew they still weren't thrilled about the situation. Oh, they were polite and friendly to him, but that's because they were decent people. And because they knew he was decent, too. But if he'd been decent *and* Asian, Peter suspected the Changs would have been a whole lot happier.

"Why?" Peter asked now. "What did your parents say about your job?"

"Almost exactly the same thing you just said," Hope admitted reluctantly. "That they couldn't understand why I'd want to spend my vacation working in a crazy department store."

"That's really something," Peter chuckled. "I never thought your parents and I would see eye to eye on anything."

Hope sighed impatiently but didn't say anything. Her parents' reaction hadn't surprised her at all, but she couldn't help feeling disappointed in Peter. He seemed to think she was the same stick-in-the-mud Hope that everyone else did. All she'd done was get a job, after all. But people were acting like she'd decided to quit school and become a rock groupie or something. Was she that dull?

Hearing Hope's sigh, Peter suddenly felt confused. He knew he wasn't the most experienced guy in the world when it came to reading girls' moods, but he thought he knew Hope pretty well. Now he wasn't so sure. She was obviously extremely touchy about this job, but why?

He started to ask, and then changed his mind. You've already done something wrong, he told himself, so just keep your mouth shut and don't push it.

With about as much finesse as an ox, Peter switched the conversation back to Rob Ladd and the squad. It wasn't what he wanted to talk about, but at least it was safe. And it seemed to work. By the time he kissed Hope good-night at her front door, she was smiling again.

But after he drove away, Peter still felt confused. He thought he knew Hope, but maybe he didn't. Or maybe he just didn't know girls at all. Was it because his parents were divorced and he lived with his mother? Did not having a father around to talk to make that much difference?

Just then, Sean Dubrow's red Fiero passed by, going toward Tara's house, and Peter smiled wryly to himself. Sean was in the exact opposite situation from Peter's — his mother was dead, and he lived with his father. Not that Peter wanted to change places with Sean — the thought actually made him shudder — but he had to admit that when it came to handling girls, Sean was miles ahead of him.

At that moment, Sean was feeling miles out of his depth. It was one thing to play your cards close to your vest, but what did you do when somebody called you and you had to show your hand?

Ever since they'd left The Pizza Palace, Tara had been talking about Sean's party, which was only three days away. That was no problem. The whole squad was invited, including Tara. But she was talking like she was his date, and that *was* a problem. If he told her now that Lisa Hutton was his cohost, how would she react? Tara could be as unpredictable as the weather, and Sean didn't want to get caught in a storm.

"What kind of food are you having?" Tara asked. "Maybe I could bring something."

"Huh? Oh, no, that's okay," Sean told her. "Dad and I talked Windy into fixing some stuff." Windy was Mrs. Windsor, the woman who cleaned house and made dinner for the two Dubrow men. "It's going to be pretty simple anyway —pretzels and dip, some sandwiches." Actually,

Lisa was supplying a lot of the food, and Sean felt himself sinking deeper into the hole he'd dug.

"Listen," he said, wanting to change the subject, "what do you think about what the coach did? It's crazy, right?"

"Mmm," Tara agreed absentmindedly. Her mind was still on the party, trying to figure out what to wear. Everything in her closet had been seen, at least twice, by every boy who was going to be there. Then she remembered Rob Ladd. "By the way," she said innocently, "are you going to invite the newest member of the squad?"

"What? No way!" Sean frowned and turned the wheel sharply, heading down Tara's street. "I said before, I don't think he should be on the squad, and besides, I hardly know the guy."

Tara twisted one of her fiery curls around her finger and smiled to herself. It was obvious that Sean was jealous of Rob Ladd, and that would make having Rob on the squad even more interesting. Interesting for Tara, anyway, who enjoyed fireworks.

"Oh, well, it *is* your party," she said sweetly, as Sean pulled up in front of the Armstrong's white Colonial house. "What about music? If you need records or tapes, I've got dozens."

"Thanks, I'll check and let you know." Now we're back to the party, Sean thought desperately. How had he gotten himself into this?

Then, as he walked with Tara up the brick path to her wreath-covered front door, Sean decided it was a waste of time to worry. Isn't that what his father always said? "Don't bother figuring out how you got into a mess, not while you're in it, anyway. Concentrate on how to get out."

Grinning down at Tara, Sean felt his old self-confidence coming back strong. For one thing, on a scale of one to ten, this mess only rated about a two. And for another, he had no doubt that he could get out of it. He always did, didn't he?

CHAPTER

By the next morning, Sean wasn't looking to get out of a mess, he was just looking to get out.

Sundays are the pits, he thought, putting his breakfast plate in the dishwasher. Windy didn't come in on weekends, and by Sunday morning the house looked like a cyclone had hit it.

Padding restlessly into the living room, Sean pushed the Sunday papers aside and flopped down on the long leather couch. What was the best way to get through the day?

No cheerleading practice, not on Sundays, so that was out. After last night's announcement about Rob Ladd, he didn't feel much like cheerleading anyway.

No date, either. His father had one; he was upstairs now, getting ready for a drive to some lodge in the country for a late brunch with his current lady friend. Sean figured he could get a date, too, but he just wasn't in the mood. He'd have his hands full in the next two weeks, juggling parties and dates and girls' feelings.

"Hey, ho!" Mark Dubrow, pulling a vivid green turtleneck over his head, joined Sean in the living room. "What a day, huh?"

"Sure is, Dad," Sean agreed, looking, for the first time, out the windows at the crisp blue sky. "Perfect driving weather."

"You said it!" Sean's father rubbed his hands together in anticipation. "Hey, what do you have on for today?"

"Nothing yet." It was funny, Sean thought, how his father sometimes acted more like the kid in the family, always on the go, working hard and playing hard.

"Taking a day of rest, huh?" Mark Dubrow cocked an eyebrow at his son and grinned. "Well, you've earned it, especially after last night's game. Wish I could have made it, but it took me a full-course dinner to nail down that order." Sean's father worked as a salesman for Tarenton Fabricators, and his job often included wooing clients over expensive meals. "I'll bet you guys looked terrific."

"Yeah, we did, as a matter of fact," Sean said. He wished his father could have seen them, too, but he understood about the job. It kept food on the table and clothes on their backs, right?

"Speaking of looking terrific," Sean said, feeling some of his energy return, "I just decided how to kill the afternoon." He'd remembered that sweater at Langston's, and he'd also remembered that this was Hope's first day there. Why not check out the sweater again, say hi to Hope, maybe even buy the sweater if the discount was good enough? He had a party coming up, and he wanted to look good for it. Besides, the mall would be packed — he could check out the girls, too.

Shoving himself off the couch, Sean headed for the stairs. "Catch you later, Dad. Have a great time!"

Mrs. Velma Randolph, a ten-year veteran of Langston's Department Store, drew herself up to her full height of just under six feet, and extended a long, red-nailed finger toward the scarf table. "Just look at that, Miss Chang," she directed in a voice that was obviously used to issuing commands.

Hope looked. Mufflers and scarves were scattered and twisted all over the table like a nest of fluffy, colorful snakes.

"It's a mess, isn't it?" Without waiting for an answer, Mrs. Randolph pointed her accusing finger at the hat table. "And that isn't any better. It's a wonder to me how customers can be so inconsiderate as to paw through the merchandise and then not bother to straighten it out."

Hope nodded, even though the mess didn't bother her nearly as much as it bothered Mrs.

Randolph. It was the Christmas rush, after all. But since this tall, gray-haired woman was her boss, Hope decided to keep her opinions to herself.

"However," Mrs. Randolph went on, "since the customer is almost always right, it's up to us to clean up after them, and make sure they can find what they're looking for." Peering down her long nose, she studied Hope with eyes that were the color of slate. "I've put you on scarves, hats, and gloves, Miss Chang, because you're only temporary, and this area doesn't require such a vast knowledge of the merchandise. Everything's out in the open, you see."

Sniffing in distaste at the two display tables, Mrs. Randolph swept her way toward the cash register counter. Hope followed, feeling like a dog being made to heel.

"Now, are you sure, Miss Chang, that you understand how to ring up a sale?"

"Oh, yes," Hope said confidently, "I'm positive I won't have any trouble."

"Hmm." Mrs. Randolph obviously had doubts, but she kept them to herself. "Well, then, since there are no customers here at the moment, I suggest you get busy straightening the tables."

When she was finally gone, Hope let out a sigh of relief. The job didn't seem like it was going to be hard at all — tiring, maybe, not hard — but if she had to work with Mrs. Randolph breathing down her neck, Hope had a feeling it wouldn't be much fun.

Now that the ice lady was out of sight, though, Hope set to work eagerly, folding mufflers and putting the knit hats into neat, color-coordinated piles. Two customers made purchases, and Hope handled the cash register without a hitch. A dozen more shoppers appeared, swooping down on the hats and scarves like birds attacking a pile of refuse, and left the tables in a bigger mess than before. Hope straightened them up again, feeling a little like the man in the myth who kept pushing a stone uphill only to have it roll back down before it reached the top.

Don't think like that, she told herself. You didn't take this job because it was going to be a mental challenge. You took it because you wanted to show everybody that you weren't who they thought you were. You wanted them to see that you could get out and do something and be a part of things, just like everybody else.

Besides, Hope thought, grabbing a handful of mufflers off the floor before they got trampled, it's twelve-thirty on a Sunday afternoon. If you weren't here, where would you be?

Almost exactly the same thought was going through Tara's mind as she stared glumly into her nearly empty closet. For the past half hour, she'd been pulling out and trying on every skirt, blouse, and pair of pants that she owned, trying to come up with the perfect outfit to wear to Sean's party.

Now her bed was piled so high with rejected clothes that its lavender down comforter was completely hidden from view, and Tara's hair was a mass of red tangles from having been tugged through so many turtleneck sweaters.

Usually, Tara wouldn't spend so much time and energy fretting about what to wear. She could go for months without wearing the same thing twice, and even if she hadn't had so many clothes, she was a wizard at putting the right touch on an outfit — a bright scarf, a bunch of narrow belts wrapped around her waist, a pair of feathered earrings that grazed her shoulders.

But there was something about Sean's party that made Tara nervous. She wasn't sure why. Maybe it was because of the way Sean had acted the night before. Whenever she'd mentioned the party, he'd either clammed up or changed the subject—which wasn't like Sean at all. He never missed a chance to blow his own horn, and she'd expected him to be bragging about how this party was going to go down as the best bash in the history of Tarenton.

Sean was trying to hide something, all of Tara's instincts told her that. And if there were any secrets around, Tara wanted to be in on them. When she wasn't, that meant she wasn't in control. And when she wasn't in control, she got nervous and tried on clothes.

"Tara?" Emily Armstrong, Tara's beautifully groomed, auburn-haired mother, stood in the doorway, a slight frown puckering her smooth forehead. "Whatever are you doing, darling? Getting ready for a clothing drive?"

Tara shook her head and laughed. "No, Mother. I know this sounds silly, but I'm having trouble finding the perfect outfit for a party."

To Mrs. Armstrong, whose wardrobe was as vast as her daughter's, the statement didn't sound silly at all. "I know exactly how you feel, sweetie," she commiserated. "Why don't you do what I always do in this situation? Buy something."

Tara smiled. It was almost a philosophy in the Armstrong family: If you have a problem, throw money at it. Fortunately, her father, Joseph, made an excellent living as a lawyer, and they were able to use that solution almost every time they needed it. Her mother hated housework, so they had Marie, a live-in housekeeper. Her father liked to keep in shape, but he liked to do it in style, so they had memberships in the country club, the riding club, the tennis club, and probably half a dozen other clubs that Tara didn't even know about.

Tara knew that money couldn't do everything. Money hadn't made her a Varsity Cheerleader or a good student, for example. But it sure was nice to have and even nicer to spend. Especially when you were nervous. There was nothing worse than sitting around in your bedroom on a Sunday afternoon, when you could be out spending money. And thanks to an almost embarrassingly generous allowance, she had plenty.

"I think I'll do just that," she told her mother now. "I haven't finished all my Christmas shopping, anyway, and Hope Chang has a job at Langston's, so I think I'll just drop in and see how she's doing."

Stepping gracefully into a pair of designer jeans, Tara grinned at her mother. "Of course, as long as I'm there, I might as well take a look in the junior department, too!"

As if they'd planned it down to the last minute, which they hadn't, the entire Varsity Squad had somehow managed to congregate around the scarves, hats, and gloves tables at exactly the same moment.

For Hope, the timing couldn't have been worse. The first hour of her job had gone smoothly, but after that — well, there was no other word for it but chaos. She'd goofed with the cash register, not once or twice, but five times. And every time, not only were the customers waiting eight deep, but Mrs. Randolph just *happened* to appear from nowhere. She didn't help at all. She just looked on in icy silence, which made Hope extremely nervous, and made her forget where the extra merchandise was kept. So the tables were almost empty at one point, and Mrs. Randolph broke her silence and chewed Hope out.

Just when Hope felt like she'd finally gotten things under control again, the cheerleaders had descended like a swarm of long-lost relatives, wanting to know how she'd been doing.

Peter was there, trying to stay out of Hope's

way and talk to her at the same time. He wasn't succeeding at either one.

Jessica, who had most of her shopping done already, had used it as an excuse just to get out of the house. Her stepfather, Daniel, had been grumbling about money again, and Jessica couldn't bear the thought of spending the afternoon listening to her mother apologize for how much things cost.

Olivia was there, looking for a hat for David. She hadn't had any luck, so she'd decided to get one for herself, which brought her to Hope's department.

Sean, his new sweater in a shopping bag, was wishing he'd never even heard of Langston's. Thanks to Lisa Hutton, who had also chosen that day to go shopping, Tara had found out that Lisa was Sean's cohost. Tara was pretending she didn't care, but Sean knew she did. He also knew she'd figure out a way to turn the tables on him.

That thought hadn't entered Tara's mind. Not yet, anyway. At the moment, all she cared about was proving to Sean that she was above being humiliated. But it wasn't easy. She kept telling herself that Sean wasn't her full-time boyfriend, that she didn't even want a full-time boyfriend.

Still, to have to listen to Lisa — petite, blonde, honey-tongued Lisa — chatter away about *their* party while Tara was stuck with her in the dressing room was humiliating.

To cover up her feelings, Tara grabbed a pink and purple muffler from the table, wrapped it around her neck, and struck a dramatic pose. "How's this?" she asked the group. "Is it me?"

Without waiting for an answer, she did a small pirouette in the aisle, colliding with Hope, who was picking up what felt like her thousandth scarf from the floor.

"Sorry," Tara said, moving out of Hope's way.

"That's okay." It wasn't really, but Hope had been taught to be polite, and besides, she wasn't really annoyed with Tara. Just with the situation. Hope knew, she just knew, that Mrs. Randolph was lurking somewhere close by. And if she peered around one of the evergreen-wrapped pillars and saw the five cheerleaders standing around getting in the customers' way, she'd blame Hope.

If Mrs. Randolph would just stay away until they go, Hope thought, glancing around nervously.

Olivia caught the look and was pretty sure what it meant. This was Hope's first day on the job and here they all were, watching her. She must think we've come to check up on her, Olivia thought.

Being watched closely was a familiar feeling to Olivia. Once she'd been a weak, sickly little girl with serious heart problems. She was fine now; it was her mother who'd never recovered. Mrs. Evans watched her only child like a hawk.

We can't do that to Hope, Olivia thought. She'd never tell us to get lost, even if we were driving her crazy, which I think we are.

45

"Hey, you guys," Olivia called out. "We've got practice tomorrow morning, in case anybody's forgotten."

"So?" Sean was glad for the chance to stop thinking about the mess he'd created for himself. "What are you suggesting, Captain? That we go home and get a good night's rest?"

Grinning, Olivia sauntered over to him, hands on her hips. "That's exactly what I'm suggesting, squad member. You don't have to go to bed right away, of course, but if anybody comes in droopy-eyed, Mrs. Engborg will really let us have it."

"She's already let us have it," Jessica said quietly.

They all knew what she meant. They hadn't forgotten, they'd just pushed it to the back of their minds. But now it came rushing back to the front. Tomorrow wasn't only the first day of practice during vacation — it was the first day of practice with Robinson Ladd.

CHAPTER

At nine-thirty on Monday morning, Ardith Engborg sat on a bleacher, once again facing her squad of six Varsity Cheerleaders. They didn't look relaxed or refreshed, as they had right after the game Saturday night. Instead, they looked confused and slightly angry, and she didn't blame them at all. She was nervous about their reaction to what she had to tell them, and she just hoped that when she was finished talking, she'd still *have* a Varsity Squad.

"First of all," she told the assembled group, "I want to thank you for coming here half an hour early. I changed the time because I wanted to talk to the six of you before Rob Ladd arrives."

Standing up, Mrs. Engborg stepped off the bleachers and onto the floor. "What I have to say isn't going to be easy," she went on, "but I know you were shocked when I decided to put Rob on the squad, and I feel I owe you an explanation."

Seated in a semicircle, the cheerleaders stared expectantly at their coach. Forgotten, for the moment, were their worries about clothes and jobs and parties and romances. Finally, they were going to get some answers to the questions they'd been asking.

"I told you that I 'decided' to put Rob Ladd on the squad, but that isn't quite true," Ardith said. "It was my decision, but it wasn't my idea. I simply felt it was the only way out, if I wanted to *keep* the Varsity Squad."

Sean frowned and started to say something, but the coach cut him off.

"I know I'm not making much sense," she said with a slight smile. "You just want the facts, right?"

"Right," Sean agreed.

"All right, here they are." Mrs. Engborg took a deep breath, seemed to gather her thoughts, and then began talking again.

"Robinson Ladd tried out for the squad last year," she said. "He didn't make it. I just naturally assumed that was the end of it. But about two weeks ago, I got a call from Judson Abbott, a young local politician who also happens to have close ties to the Ladd family, especially to Rob's father, Senator Ladd."

"In other words," Sean put in, "Abbott's a brownie."

48

Another small smile from Mrs. Engborg. "Sean," she told him, "listen to what I have to say. Then you can comment. Agreed?"

Sean nodded reluctantly. "Agreed."

"Mr. Abbott told me that Rob was extremely disappointed about not making the squad, and that since Senator Ladd was away from home so often, Rob had confided in him — Mr. Abbott. It seems that Mr. Abbott is something of a father figure to Rob."

"All right," Olivia remarked, "so Rob was disappointed. A lot of kids were. Why does *he* all of a sudden get his wish?"

"I'm coming to that," the coach said sharply. "I just want to make sure you know all the facts."

"Sorry," Olivia mumbled.

Mrs. Engborg relented. "It's all right. I don't blame you for being impatient." Running her fingers through her short blonde hair, she took another deep breath. "My response to Mr. Abbott was almost exactly the same as yours, Olivia," she continued. "But he's nothing if not persistent. And over the next few days, he called me repeatedly, asking me to put Rob on the squad. I kept telling him it was impossible, and I think he finally believed me. That's when he changed his tactics."

"What do you mean?" Peter asked.

"I mean that he started playing dirty," the coach said bluntly. "Last week, he came by the school and told me in so many words that if I wanted Tarenton High to have a Varsity Squad

49

at all, then that squad had better include Rob Ladd."

"How could he say that?" Jessica asked.

"Yeah," Tara chimed in. "Who is he, anyway?"

"I think I know," Hope said. "Remember? Sean told us he was on the school board." She looked at Mrs. Engborg. "Judson Abbott threatened you, didn't he?"

Everyone started talking at once, wanting to know what Hope meant, but Mrs. Engborg quieted them with a clap of her hands. "Hope's right," she said. "Abbott threatened me. He didn't come right out and say it — that's not his style. But he hinted that if I didn't go along with him, that he'd use his influence with the school board to cut funding for what he called 'fluff' activities, like cheerleading."

"Fluff!" Tara exclaimed indignantly. "I'd like to see him do a few handsprings and walkovers and call it fluff!"

"Naturally, I agree with you," Mrs. Engborg told her. "Unfortunately, we're in a minority. Most people see cheerleading as just a fun thing to do, a real *extra*curricular activity. And if Judson Abbott starts talking like that to the school board, he could get them on his side. Believe me, he's a very persuasive young man."

"Who's really behind this?" Peter wanted to know. "Rob? Or his father?"

"Both, I'll bet," Sean muttered. "Some people call it politics, but the real word for it is blackmail."

"That's exactly what it is," Mrs. Engborg admitted. "As to who's behind it, I'm not sure. Rob and his father might know nothing of Abbott's tactics."

"Rob knows, I'd bet money on it," Sean said.

"How can you say that?" Tara asked. "He might be completely innocent."

"Come on, Tara. The guy doesn't make the squad, so he goes crying to Daddy. Only Daddy isn't there, so he tells Abbott and Abbott says, Don't worry, kid, I'll fix things for you." Shaking his head, Sean gave a disgusted laugh. "You think Rob doesn't have any idea how he all of a sudden got on the squad? He has to know! And I'll bet Senator Ladd knows, too."

Privately, Ardith agreed with Sean, at least about Rob. She wasn't sure about the senator, but it didn't really matter. "The point is," she said, "Judson Abbott has me over a barrel."

"But why can't you just tell somebody what he's done?" Olivia burst out in frustration.

Jessica nodded. "Wouldn't that make him back off?"

"I thought of that," Mrs. Engborg said. "But when I suggested it to Mr. Abbott, he said he'd simply deny it. He also hinted that if I talked, he'd make sure that cheerleading funds would be cut back."

"I see what you mean about that barrel," Peter remarked.

"Right." Mrs. Engborg began pacing back and forth in front of the group. "This isn't fair, of course. But what I'm asking you to do is to go along with me on this."

"It isn't fair that it happened at all," Hope commented.

"You're right, Hope. But at the moment, I don't see any way out. I want to keep the squad together, and if the rest of you agree, then we'll just have to play by the new rules." The coach stopped pacing and faced her cheerleaders. "What do you say?"

Everyone was quiet for a moment, exchanging glances. There were shock and frustration in their eyes, but not a hint of doubt about what they were going to do. They'd stick with their coach.

"We're with you, Mrs. Engborg," Olivia said firmly. "Did you think we wouldn't be?"

Ardith smiled. "No. But I felt I had to ask. It's a terrible situation, I know, but I have confidence in you. You'll — we'll — make the best of it." She paused again, then went on. "I'm not proud of myself for caving in," she said softly. "But I'm very proud of you for understanding. Now," she went on briskly, "there's just one last thing: Keep everything I've told you under your hats. Not a word about it to anyone."

No one needed to be told that. The squad was in jeopardy, and they'd do everything they could to protect it, including keeping their mouths shut.

Mrs. Engborg turned to sit down again, and as she did, a figure appeared in the doorway. He was dressed in raggedy gray sweat pants, scruffy sneakers, and a faded blue sweat shirt cut off just above the elbows. As the squad watched, Robinson Ladd gave them a smile that didn't quite reach his pale blue eyes, and began moving into the gym.

He's got a nice walk, Tara thought, watching the graceful way Rob moved his lean but well-muscled body. Maybe he'll turn out to be a natural. That would be perfect.

Look at the guy, Sean thought darkly. He's dressed like a ragpicker. What's he trying to do — prove he's one of the gang?

The others watched Rob, too, unable to think of a thing to say to him. He was the enemy; they could hardly welcome him with open arms. But he was also a part of them now. They'd agreed to it.

If Rob was uncomfortable with the squad's scrutiny, he didn't show it. He moved easily, as if he belonged, and he didn't avoid their eyes. When he was a few feet from them, he stopped, and still smiling, raised his arm to look at his watch. Sean noticed that the watch didn't exactly go with Rob's "dressed-down" look — it must have cost at least five hundred dollars.

"Looks like I'll have to trade this baby in," Rob said, tapping the watch. "I thought I was early, but I see you all are way ahead of me." He brushed his pale brown hair back off his forehead and grinned. "Let's see how fast I can catch up."

* * *

"Olivia, you look flushed. Are you sick?" Mrs. Evans reached a hand across the dinner table, ready to feel Olivia's forehead, but Olivia managed to evade it by pushing her chair back and standing up.

"I feel fine, Mother," she said, stacking her plates together. "It's just kind of hot in here."

"Hot?" Though Mrs. Evans was solidly built, she complained of the cold, and always wore an extra sweater in the wintertime. "It's December. It's twenty-five degrees outside. How can you say it's hot?"

Mr. Evans looked up from his dish of chocolate pudding. "I'm a little warm myself," he said mildly. "The dining room's the hottest room in the house."

Mrs. Evans rolled her eyes and sighed loudly, but she didn't say any more, and Olivia bit her lips to keep from grinning. Her father used to agree with everything his wife said, but Olivia had noticed that lately he'd changed his style. He didn't argue or get angry; he just quietly said what he thought, especially on the subject of his daughter's health.

When it came to convincing her mother that she wasn't ready for intensive care, Olivia appreciated any ally she could get, and as she picked up her father's plate, she kissed him on the cheek. "I'm really fine, Mother," she said again. "And I know you want to watch that special on television, so I'll clean up the kitchen."

Once her parents were settled in front of the television set, Olivia shut the kitchen door and breathed a sigh of relief. For once, her mother had been right. Olivia *wasn't* feeling well, but it wasn't because she was sick. Physically, she was fine. But mentally — that was another story.

What have we gotten ourselves into? she wondered, as she began scraping the plates. We told Mrs. Engborg that we'd go along and make everything work out. It was so easy to say. But that was before we saw Rob Ladd in action.

Action? Olivia opened the dishwasher and almost laughed. Action was definitely the wrong word. What was the right one? Disaster, that was it. As a cheerleader, Rob Ladd was a disaster. He couldn't do a stag leap, he couldn't do a split, he could barely do a forward roll, and there was no way Olivia was going to trust him with the split-second timing that some of their routines required.

I can just see it now, she thought, grimly shoving the plates into the dishwasher. I come cartwheeling across the floor, expecting to find him in place, ready to lift me to his shoulders. He lifts, pushes too hard, and I go sprawling backward onto my head. Mother would *really* have something to worry about then!

The only thing Rob had done successfully during that morning's practice was clap his hands with the right timing. Big deal. So he could clap his hands. With a little practice, maybe he'll be

55

able to stamp his feet without breaking one of his toes.

And the worst part, Olivia fumed, pouring soap into the dishwasher and slamming its door shut, was his attitude! She thought he'd be totally humiliated. *She*, for one, would have crawled into a hole for at least a week, if she'd been in the same situation.

But not Robinson Ladd. Either he didn't know how bad he was, which didn't seem possible, or he had the thickest skin of any human she'd ever met. All his goofs, all his falls, seemed to roll right off him, like water from a duck's back. He'd just say, smiling that stingy smile of his, "Guess I need a little work on that one," or "I think I'll practice this one in my spare time," or, worse, "Hey, I think I'm getting the hang of it now."

Getting the hang of it? Wishing it were Rob's neck, Olivia twisted the full garbage bag closed and wrapped a tie around it. Somebody was getting hanged, all right — the squad. If Rob Ladd's going to be on it, then we'll have to change all our routines. We'll wind up doing simple rah-rah stuff that any idiot could do.

Just when we were getting good, Olivia thought. Just when we were a team, this has to happen!

Olivia was wrapping the leftovers when the phone rang. Munching on a carrot stick, she reached for the phone, answered it, and heard a male voice say, "Miss Evans, this is the Triple D

Investigative Agency. We'd like to ask you a few questions, if you don't mind."

Grinning, Olivia chomped down on the carrot. "I'm not sure," she said. "What did you say the agency's name is?"

"Three-D. That's D as in diligent, determined, and, uh. . . ."

". . . demented," Olivia finished with a laugh.

"Oh, then you *have* heard of us." David Duffy laughed, too, and dropped his "official" tone. "How ya doing, Livvy? *What* are you doing, besides crunching something in my ear?"

"Sorry." Olivia swallowed quickly. "It was a raw carrot. Impossible to chew quietly. I was cleaning up the kitchen," she said, deciding not to answer his first question. If she said she was fine, she'd be lying, but if she said she wasn't, David would want to know why. And Olivia couldn't tell him.

"Cleaning the kitchen — that sounds exciting," David commented. "Now, how'd it go?"

"How'd what go?" Olivia asked, knowing exactly what he meant.

"Practice. Your first practice with Robinson Ladd."

"Oh. Well, it was a little . . . rocky." That's the understatement of the year, Olivia thought wryly. "You know, he has to learn the routines and stuff. It'll take a while." Like forever.

"A while. huh?" David said. "You've only got . . . what? Two and a half, three weeks till the next game. Can you get it together by then?"

"We don't have a choice." That was the truth, at least.

David whistled softly. "Looks like you've got your work cut out for you. So what about why he's on the squad? Did Mrs. Engborg break her silence and tell you?"

"Um. . . ." Olivia was trying to think of what to say without actually lying, when her mother came into the kitchen and began rummaging in the refrigerator. Bottles clanked noisily as Mrs. Evans searched for something to munch on, and Olivia took advantage of it. Lowering her voice, she said, "David? This isn't the best time to talk."

"Right," David said, immediately understanding. "I've got ears. Your mother's not going to find what she's looking for until you're off the phone."

Olivia stifled a giggle and tried not to look at her mother. "You guessed it."

"Okay. Well, I wish we were together right now, Livvy," he told her. "But I'll see you tomorrow and you can give me the lowdown, okay?"

"The lowdown?"

"Sure. The 'inside story' on why Robinson Ladd is suddenly on Tarenton High's Varsity Squad, remember?"

How could I forget? Olivia thought. Aloud, she simply said, "Sure. I'll see you tomorrow, David. 'Bye."

At least you didn't lie to him, she told herself as she left the kitchen and went to her bedroom.

But how long can you keep that up? David will ask the same questions tomorrow, and what will you tell him? Mrs. Engborg said to keep it under your hat, and it's just your luck that your boyfriend is a reporter.

Sighing, Olivia flopped down on her bed, almost crushing a shopping bag. She pushed the bag aside, and then sat up, checking to make sure she hadn't done any damage.

Inside the bag was David's Christmas present. She hadn't found it at Langston's or any of the trendy boutiques she'd visited. She'd found it in a secondhand store that she'd wandered into that afternoon, not really expecting to find anything.

But there it had been, stuck on one of the shelves, gathering dust. The minute she saw it, Olivia knew it was absolutely perfect.

She pulled it out of the bag now, and smiled. It was still perfect. A hat, but not just any old hat. Checkered in pale gray and green wool, with two ear flaps that tied on top, and sloping brims in the front and back, it was an almost exact replica of every Sherlock Holmes hat she'd ever seen.

A Sherlock Holmes hat, Olivia thought wryly. Maybe it wasn't such a good idea, after all. With this hat on his head, David Duffy would never stop asking questions about Robinson Ladd.

CHAPTER

The next morning, Tarenton's Christmas card weather of sparkling snow, bright sun, and blue skies underwent a drastic change. The snow was still there, but the blue sky and sun were gone, hidden behind a thick mass of gray clouds that seemed to press down on the town, and on everyone's spirits. It was still cold, but not the kind of crisp, inviting cold that everyone enjoyed. Instead, people hurried from building to building, or from house to car, complaining of heating bills and worrying just how much more snow that gray mass was going to dump on them.

The weather inside the Tarenton High gym had changed, too, and not for the better. As the seven Varsity Cheerleaders went through their warm-up exercises, Olivia couldn't help noticing that the relaxed, friendly atmosphere she'd felt a week ago was missing. There was no joking, no teasing, no laughter. There was almost no talking. Just seven people grimly stretching their muscles with about as much enthusiasm as prison inmates.

The night before, Olivia had thought the whole thing through, tossing and turning on her bed the entire time, and decided that no matter how bad Rob was, they'd have to live with him. Of course, they'd try to make him better, but if he was a lost cause, then so be it. He was one of them now, and they'd promised Mrs. Engborg that they'd make the best of a rotten situation.

Olivia glanced over at Rob. He was doing sit-ups, and he was doing them very well. He didn't look like a klutz at all doing sit-ups. Too bad we can't use them in one of our routines, she thought with a sigh.

"Okay," Mrs. Engborg called out, breaking into Olivia's thoughts. "I think you're all limber enough. Let's try 'Red and White.' I've changed it to make it work for seven people instead of six, so we'll walk through it a few times to get the hang of it."

The "Red and White" cheer was an old stand-by; six of the cheerleaders knew it like the backs of their hands, and quickly got into position for it. Normally, it consisted of Hope and Peter, and Tara and Sean chanting and doing a jazzy dance step, while Olivia and Jessica whirled around them in a series of gymnastic moves that included

61

handsprings and back walkovers. The routine ended with Olivia and Jessica standing on the guys' shoulders, while Tara and Hope did splits on either side.

Now, Mrs. Engborg told them that there would be no shoulder stands. Instead, the guys would do stag leaps and the girls would do splits.

It won't be quite as flashy, Olivia thought, but it'll still have plenty of zip. *If* Rob can handle it. As they walked through the steps she knew so well, Olivia glanced up into the bleachers and spotted Patrick Henley and Pres Tilford. Pres was a former cheerleader; now he and Patrick were in the moving business together. They must have dropped by on the way to a job, she thought, returning Pres's wave. She knew it hadn't been Pres's idea to come by, though. Oh, he liked to keep up with the squad, but he wasn't a fanatic about it. It was Patrick who couldn't stay away.

Smiling to herself, Olivia glanced over at Jessica. She was the reason Patrick was here. He was crazy about her, that was obvious. But, as usual, Jessica was concentrating on cheerleading, not on the people watching.

Olivia ordered herself to do the same thing, but just then, two more people came into the gym and climbed onto the bleachers. The first one, racing cap in hand, was David Duffy. Olivia's heart sank. Not that she wasn't happy to see him, but she knew he'd probably stick around and ask her a bunch of questions when practice was over. She'd managed to get out of answering any of them last night, but she didn't know how long she could keep that up.

She didn't recognize the second person until he turned and sat down, and then she saw that it was Judson Abbott. It was bad enough that he'd created this mess, she thought angrily, did he have to come and gloat over it, too?

Judson Abbott wasn't looking at Olivia, but she gave him an icy stare anyway. It didn't make her feel any better, so she decided to ignore everything but the routine they were working on.

"All right," Mrs. Engborg said after a few more minutes, "let's try it. Take it slow, though. Once I'm sure it's working, we'll have a real run-through."

> "Red and White,
> You're all right!
> Give that team. . . ."

Only five steps into the routine, it became obvious that Rob was completely out of sync with the rest of them. The dance steps weren't that difficult, but a sense of timing was important, and Rob didn't seem to have one. He was either way ahead or way behind, and when they were all supposed to whirl to the left, he whirled to the right, crashing into Jessica, who lost her balance and bumped into Peter, who slid into Sean.

"Not a bad pile-up, considering I wasn't even trying for one," Rob joked.

Nobody laughed.

"From the top," Mrs. Engborg called out.

> "Red and White,
> You're all right!
> Give that team
> A roaring fight!
> Red and White. . . ."

This time, they got through ten steps before Rob goofed. Amazingly, he didn't seem embarrassed. He just got in place again, an amused smile on his lips. His skin must be as thick as an alligator's, Olivia thought. She knew she should offer to help him. Hadn't she decided that they'd have to do everything they could to make this work? Besides, she was the captain, and it was up to the captain to set the example.

Gritting her teeth, Oliva started to walk over to Rob, but before she could move, Mrs. Engborg spoke.

"I think we can make this work," she said, looking up from the paper she'd been scribbling on, "if we simplify the opening steps. There's really no need for all the side steps and twirling; it'll work just as well if you keep up a steady stamping. Let's try it."

Wordlessly, the cheerleaders took their places again, and out of the corner of her eye, Olivia saw David lean forward. He was watching them closely, frowning, as if he couldn't quite understand what was happening.

Six members of the squad knew what was happening — they were trapped. Stuck with Rob Ladd, they were going to have to simplify every routine just to suit him. If jumping up and down and screaming could have changed things, the gym would have been filled with noise. Instead, the squad finished its practice in near-total silence.

"I was afraid of this," Jessica said quietly. She pulled a rust-colored sweater over her head and raked her fingers through her long hair. "I knew something like this would happen, but I didn't know it was going to be this bad."

"I didn't." Hope sat on one of the benches in the girls' locker room and tugged on her boots. "I knew it would take a while for Rob to catch on to our routines, but I guess I was just being optimistic."

"Optimistic is right," Olivia agreed. "That guy's never going to catch on!"

"Well. . . ." Tara unwrapped a towel from around her head and shook out her damp curls. "Don't get me wrong, now. I know he's not Varsity material, but he did manage to get through the routine once Mrs. Engborg changed it."

"Tara" — Jessica began stuffing her warm-up clothes into her nylon duffel bag — "a three-year old could have gotten through that routine."

Tara, stepping into a pair of tight green stirrup pants, decided not to argue, mainly because Jessica was right. The routine *was* extremely simple. But even though Rob wasn't the greatest cheerleader on earth, she still found him very attractive.

She'd been next to him during practice, and she'd taken the opportunity to have a good, close look at him. She liked what she saw, and she wanted to find out what was behind that mysterious half smile he wore.

Tara knew that no one was in the mood to hear how she felt about Rob, though, so she kept quiet and started brushing her hair. The others were quiet, too, putting on makeup, straightening their clothes, and packing their duffel bags.

Hope was thinking about her job. She had only fifteen minutes to get from the school to Langston's, and she'd have to hurry or Mrs. Randolph would probably dock her for every minute she was late. Peter was driving her, though, so she'd probably make it. Of course, that meant she'd only have fifteen minutes to spend with Peter. But maybe she'd see him tonight.

The locker room was steamy and the benches were hard, but Olivia lingered anyway. She hoped that by the time she left, David would be gone. She'd seen that curious look on his face at practice. He thought something funny was going on, and once David Douglas Duffy was on the trail, there was no stopping him. Olivia knew that. She just didn't want to deal with it right at the moment, and the thought that she was actually avoiding the boy she cared about made her feel slightly sick.

Jessica had seen Patrick and Pres leave midway through practice. By now they were probably loading the contents of someone's apartment into the van. She was glad, in a way, that Patrick was too busy to stick around. She was always so confused about him, but the afternoon loomed ahead like an empty room, and she wasn't sure how to fill it.

Well, she'd think of something. Right now, though, she wanted to know what they were going to do about Rob. "How are we going to handle this situation?" she asked, breaking the silence in the locker room.

"What do you mean?" Tara looked confused.

"I mean, there are seven cheerleaders now. Six of us are good and one is rotten. If we keep doing what we did today, then pretty soon seven of us will be rotten. I don't want that to happen."

"I don't, either, Jessica," Hope said. "But I don't think it'll get that bad. Besides, we told Mrs. Engborg that we'd go along with this."

"I'm not saying we should have a sit-down strike or anything," Jessica protested. "But I do say we shouldn't go out of our way to help Rob. Maybe if he falls on his face often enough, he'll realize how bad he is and he'll quit."

"That seems awfully cruel," Tara said.

"Maybe," Jessica agreed. "But what he's doing to us isn't exactly nice."

Olivia shook her head. "That's not the point, Jessica. The point is we promised we'd try to make this work. If we let him stumble along like a lame duck, we'll be letting Mrs. Engborg down. Plus," she added with a grin, "the coach would never let us get away with it."

67

"So what are you saying?" Jessica asked, slinging her bag over her shoulder. "That we put in extra hours, helping Rob learn his left foot from his right?"

"No. I guess . . . I don't know." Olivia zipped her burgundy down jacket and shook her head again. "I'm not asking you or anybody to help him out. Unless you want to. All I want is for the squad to stick together somehow. I don't want us to fall apart."

"I don't want that, either," Jessica said. "I guess we just have different ideas on how to keep us together."

In the boys' locker room, Sean and Peter were having a similar conversation. Rob was still outside chatting with Judson Abbott, and after a quick glance at the door, Peter spoke up.

"I've been thinking," he said, as they toweled themselves dry. "We can't let Rob bring us down to his level, because it'll ruin the squad. I'm not saying we sabotage him or anything like that, but I think we're going to have to let him fend for himself. If he can't keep up, that's his problem, not ours."

"Wait a minute, back up," Sean said, pulling on a pair of jeans. "I caught the word *sabotage* in there somewhere."

"Yeah, well, the idea did cross my mind," Peter admitted.

"It's brilliant!" Sean grinned and his eyes began to sparkle. "Just what kind of sabotage were you thinking of?"

"I told you, it crossed my mind," Peter protested. "But that's all. I mean, we can't really do anything to the guy."

"Yeah, I know we can't." Still grinning, Sean sat on one of the benches to pull on his socks. "But you gotta admit, it's tempting."

As he reached for his parka, Peter laughed. It was rare that he and Sean Dubrow saw eye-to-eye on anything. It actually felt good having something in common with him, even if it was mutual dislike of Rob Ladd. "I could almost feel sorry for the guy, if he didn't have an ego the size of an elephant."

"Well, I don't know," Sean said, whose ego was almost as big as Rob's, "there's nothing wrong with having a good opinion of yourself. The problem with Ladd is, he doesn't have a good self, so his opinion's all wrong."

"Well, anyway," Peter said, laughing again, "sabotage is out. And the only other thing I could come up with was what I told you — just let him go it alone and see how far he gets. I'm willing to bet he'll quit."

"I'm not." Sean's eyes darkened as he remembered Rob's superior attitude at practice, and then they lit up again. "But who knows? Maybe we'll get lucky. Maybe he'll break a leg."

At that moment, Rob Ladd entered the locker room, his presence cutting off the boys' laughter

69

like a slap in the face. Peter fished in his pockets for his gloves and car keys; Sean pulled on a clean sweat shirt.

Whistling softly, Rob removed his expensive watch, carelessly tossing it onto a bench. "I was a little surprised at practice today," he said. "I thought there'd be more of an audience."

Sean kept quiet, but Peter, in spite of his dislike for Rob, felt compelled to say something. "There's usually a small bunch of people hanging around to watch. But we're on vacation, and I guess they've got better things to do."

"But I wasn't talking about just 'a bunch of people,' " Rob said, smiling as if at some private joke. "Dubrow knows what I mean, don't you Dubrow?"

"He was talking about girls," Sean told Peter.

"Right you are, Dubrow. Go to the head of the class!" Chuckling, Rob draped a towel around his neck. "Considering that you're on the squad, I really expected some of your loyal following to be there."

"You mean you *hoped* they'd be there," Sean said, rising to the bait. "Right, Robinson?"

The minute he said it, he knew he should have kept his mouth shut. Rob's smile got wider, and his sandy eyebrows lifted in mock surprise. "Why, Dubrow, do I detect some worry? Are you afraid I might be cutting in on your territory?"

"Not a chance," Sean told him.

"Not a chance of what?" Rob asked. "Not a

brake hard to stop in time. Really bright. Crash the car just because some no-class jerk got the better of you. Taking a deep breath, Sean pulled slowly away from the intersection and forced himself to calm down.

He drove slowly and carefully the rest of the way to school, but his mind was still racing, trying to come up with a way to get even with Rob Ladd. Then, as he pulled into the Tarenton High parking lot, something suddenly occurred to him: He didn't have to do anything to get even. All he had to do was sit back and watch the look on Ladd's face when his loyal female following saw him trying to be a cheerleader. Their smiles would turn to sneers in about two seconds flat, and Sean, for one, couldn't wait to see it.

As he strode into the gym, Sean's cocky, self-confident walk was back, and Tara noticed it immediately. She didn't know anything about the encounter he'd had yesterday with Rob, but she did know that Sean was far from thrilled to have Rob on the squad. And she wondered just how long that cocky walk would last once he saw who was in the stands.

Casually, Tara glanced up to the bleachers, to make sure. Yes. Lisa Hutton was still there. She was sitting with two other girls, and both of them were frequent dates of Rob Ladd. Had Lisa changed cheering sections? Tara didn't know, but it was going to be fun finding out. And if she had, Tara thought, then it would serve Sean right for being so sneaky about his party.

Shifting her gaze to Sean, Tara watched as he started his warm-ups. So far, he hadn't noticed anything, and he was obviously staying as far away from Rob as possible.

Tara wasn't one to sit back and wait, not if she could get things moving herself, so she put on a bright smile and cartwheeled over to Sean. "Hi!"

"Tara, you're looking great this morning." With an appreciative grin, Sean took in Tara's orange leotard and matching sweat pants. "I can see you're not losing any sleep over the decline and fall of the Tarenton High Varsity Squad."

"I don't happen to think it's going to decline *or* fall," Tara said, "so there's nothing to lose sleep about. But I know you don't agree, so let's not talk about it."

"Fine with me." Sean didn't want to discuss Rob Ladd at all, especially not with Tara. "What's on your mind?"

"Nothing, really," Tara replied innocently. "I just wondered if you were all set for your party tonight."

Sean eyed her curiously. She couldn't have forgotten about Lisa being his co-host, he knew that. He also knew she was ticked off about it, even though she'd never admit it. So why was she acting so nice about it all of a sudden?

Come on, Dubrow, he told himself, don't be paranoid. You've got an enemy on this squad, but it isn't Tara Armstrong. Starting in on some leg stretches, Sean smiled. "Yeah," he said, "everything's set. The soda's on ice, the chips are crisp, and the house is so clean, Dad and I are practically afraid to breathe. I even hung some mistletoe," he told her, wiggling one eyebrow up and down suggestively.

"That'll make things interesting," Tara laughed. "Well, I just wanted to make sure everything was ready. If you think of anything you missed before practice is over, you can always ask Lisa. She's here, you know."

Stopping in midstretch, Sean looked up to the bleachers. Lisa Hutton wasn't hard to spot, her white-blonde hair always seemed to glow like a soft light. But Lisa's hair didn't interest Sean at the moment. What interested him was who she was with — two Robinson Ladd groupies — and who she was watching — Robinson Ladd.

So. That explained Tara's sudden sweetness about the party. Letting him know that Lisa had her eye on Rob was Tara's way of getting back at him.

Putting on an I-couldn't-care-less expression, Sean turned to say something to Tara. But she had already moved off, her red hair swinging like a fiery curtain as she moved across the gym.

It doesn't matter, Sean told himself. Let Lisa watch Rob Ladd all she wants. That glazed look of admiration will change pretty quick, once she sees the golden boy in action. Smiling confidently, Sean went on with his warm-ups until Mrs. Engborg arrived.

"All right," the coach said, without even a good-morning smile, "let's begin. We'll do 'Red and White' again, just to make sure we've got it."

Responding to the briskness in her voice, the squad members took their places quickly and silently. Even when there had been only six cheerleaders, there was never much fooling around during practice, but this time the atmosphere was positively grim. Sean was smiling, but that was only because he couldn't wait to see Rob Ladd fall flat on his face.

> "Red and White,
> You're all right!
> Give that team
> A roaring fight!
> Red and White,
> You've got the might!
> Tarenton Wolves are
> Outa sight!"

When practice was over, Sean wasn't smiling anymore. Rob had actually managed to get through the cheer without a stumble. Of course, the cheer was so simple now that anyone who knew how to walk could do it. But that didn't matter — what mattered was that Rob hadn't made a fool of himself. None of the girls watching him, including Lisa, cared that the Varsity Squad was going downhill fast. All they cared about was Rob, and they hadn't been disappointed.

Frustrated, Sean left the school without bothering to shower. He could do that at home, and besides, he didn't want to risk another locker-room run-in with Rob, which would put him in a foul mood for the rest of the day. He didn't want that, not with his party only a few hours away. At least, he thought, the guy won't be around to ruin *that*.

"I wonder what's eating him," Olivia said, as she and Jessica watched Sean stride out of the gym.

"He's jealous," Jessica said.

"Of Rob Ladd?" Olivia laughed. "Sean has more talent in his little finger than Rob has in his whole body!"

Jessica nodded. "I know. But Sean's not thinking of talent. He's thinking of girls."

"I should have guessed," Olivia said, laughing again.

The gym had emptied out by now, but the two cheerleaders stayed behind for a few minutes, talking. "Olivia," Jessica said, "I wanted to explain about yesterday, when I said I wasn't going to help Rob. I haven't changed my mind, but I don't want you to think I'm fighting you."

"Okay," Olivia told her. "But I still think we have to do everything we can to keep the squad looking good, and if that means helping Rob, then that's what we'll have to do."

Since they were on opposite sides, there didn't seem to be much more to say on the subject. They showered and changed, talking about Christmas and the Sherlock Holmes hat Olivia had found,

77

and Sean's party that night. But there was a kind of coolness between them, and that bothered Jessica. Just when the squad had started to get really good, just when it seemed like she and Olivia might actually become friends, Rob Ladd had to come along and ruin everything. Jessica still thought she was right about not letting Rob drag the squad down to his level, and she was annoyed with Olivia for being willing to let him. But mostly she was just angry at the situation.

When she stepped outside, the weather didn't do anything to change Jessica's mood. The sky was still a gun-metal gray, and the sparkling snow of a week before was splattered with mud. Wishing the clouds would either blow away or dump their load, Jessica bent her head against the cold wind and started down the school steps.

At first, she paid no attention to the honking, thinking it was just some impatient driver. But the honking went on, and finally Jessica looked to see who was making so much noise.

It was Patrick Henley, waving wildly at her from inside his moving van. Waving back, Jessica walked over to the curb and climbed in beside him.

"Are you just finishing a job or just going to one?" she asked as he pulled down the street.

"Neither," Patrick said with a laugh. "If you want to know the truth, I left Pres to deal with the phone while I went out and did a little last-minute Christmas shopping."

"Did you get everything?"

"Yep, I'm all finished," he said, thinking of the gift he'd bought for Jessica and how great it would look on her. "Hey, I'm free for the afternoon — how about going ice-skating?"

Jessica hesitated. She wasn't looking forward to going home, but she wasn't sure she wanted to go skating with Patrick. She was already going to Sean's party with him, and that seemed to be all she could handle. "Don't you have to work?" she asked.

"Nope," he said cheerfully. "Business is slow right now — not too many people want to move four days before Christmas."

"Oh, right, I didn't think of that."

Patrick decided to ignore the fact that Jessica hadn't said yes or no to the ice-skating idea. "Speaking of Christmas," he went on, still trying to sound cheerful, "we ought to pick a day to chop trees. It's a little late to get started today. So that only leaves tomorrow, Friday, and Saturday."

Jessica shifted uncomfortably. "I should have told you sooner, I guess."

"What, you already have your tree?" Patrick nodded. "Most people do, I know."

"No, we don't have it yet." Jessica thought of making up some excuse, like maybe it was a tradition that her family always picked out their tree together. But that was ridiculous. Her family didn't have any traditions, not since her mother

79

had married Daniel. Oh, they got a tree, but always at the last minute, and always with Daniel griping about what a rip-off the whole thing was.

Patrick was watching her, waiting for an answer. Jessica cleared her throat. "It really sounds like fun," she said truthfully, "but I'm afraid I won't be able to go."

"Oh. Well. It was just an idea." Patrick turned his attention back to the road, feeling disappointed. He was angry, too, he couldn't help it. If she'd just give an inch, she might find out how great they could be together. Instead, she seemed to freeze up every time she was near him, and it was beginning to bug him. A lot.

You don't need this, he told himself. Sure, she's beautiful and bright and fun, but so what? She's also obviously not interested. So why torture yourself?

"You know," he said, "I get the feeling that you don't want to go out with me at all."

Startled, Jessica's green eyes widened. "Why do you say that?"

"Because every time I ask you, you come up with an excuse. Or a nonexcuse, like 'I'm afraid I won't be able to go.' "

"That's not true," Jessica said. "I'm going out with you tonight, aren't I?"

"Oh, right, Sean's party." Patrick tightened his grip on the steering wheel. He was more angry than hurt now, and he didn't care what he said. "Are you sure you really want to? I mean, please,

Jessica, don't do me any favors. If you don't want to go with me, just say so. I can take it."

"I wouldn't have said I'd go with you if I didn't want to," Jessica told him, starting to get angry herself. "And I'm not doing you a favor. That's a rotten thing to say — you make me sound like a snob."

"I don't know *what* you are!" Patrick almost shouted. "I like you, Jess, and I thought you liked me. And when two people like each other, they want to spend time together, right? So how come I get the feeling that whenever you're with me, you wish you were someplace else?"

"I *do* like you," Jessica cried. "I just don't want to . . . to get involved!"

"With me?"

"With anybody!"

"Well, that sure sounds like fun." Pulling the van to a stop in front of Jessica's house, Patrick slumped in the seat and shook his head. "What do you have in mind, going through life with a wall around yourself?"

Jessica didn't answer.

"Okay, forget it." Patrick took a deep breath. "Maybe we should forget about going to Sean's party together, too."

"Maybe we should," Jessica said.

"Fine."

Without another word, Jessica let herself out of the van and strode up the sidewalk to her front door. She didn't look back before she went inside.

Patrick was still angry as he drove away. She doesn't want to get involved, huh? he thought furiously. What did she think *he* wanted, to get married, for Pete's sake? This relationship was turning out to be as bad as the one he'd had with Mary Ellen Kirkwood. Someone had warned him about this, he remembered suddenly. Olivia, that's who. She'd told him to be careful. Jessica wasn't interested in any kind of commitment, and Olivia was afraid that Patrick might get hurt.

Maybe Olivia should go into the fortune-telling business, Patrick though wryly. Because he *was* hurt. But he'd get over it. And once he did, he'd find somebody else. Somebody who didn't crawl into her shell whenever she heard the word love.

"This has to be one of the worst days I have ever spent in my entire life," Jessica said, "and it's not even half over."

No one answered, because no one was there. Daniel and her mother were both at work. Jessica had taken advantage of the empty house by angrily kicking off her boots and slinging her jacket onto the kitchen table. Then she'd opened the refrigerator door and immediately slammed it shut again as hard as she could.

None of the slamming and slinging had helped. She was still furious, at Patrick *and* at herself. How could she have let him get to her like that? You were only supposed to get mad if you cared, and she didn't, not that much, anyway.

Calm down, she told herself. It's not worth it. You're hurt now, but you'll get over it. And you'll start getting over it by going to Sean's party tonight. By yourself. You're not going to miss out on a good time because of some stupid fight with some boy.

Of course, Patrick wasn't just *some* boy, Jessica was honest enough to admit that. If things had been different, she would have leaped into love with him and not looked back. But things weren't different. And there was no sense in trying to make them different. You'll get over it, she told herself again.

Calmly, Jessica opened the cabinet and took out a box of crackers. Then her feelings caught up with her again, and she slammed the cabinet door shut. That didn't help, either.

CHAPTER

"More chicken, Hope?" Mrs. Chang pointed to the platter of cutlets and smiled encouragingly. "You haven't eaten much."

"Thank you, Mother, they were delicious, but I'm full." Hope smiled back and tried not to show how anxious she was to leave the table. Peter would be here to pick her up in forty-five minutes for Sean's party, and she was still in her work clothes.

"Hope, you look tired," her father commented. "That job of yours isn't turning out to be too much, is it?"

"No, Father." Hope kept smiling, but inside she cringed. Here we go again, she thought. Her parents were about to start in on why she shouldn't have taken the job, and even though she wouldn't admit it to them, she *was* tired. Too tired to defend herself.

It had been a horrible day at Langston's. As Christmas got closer and closer, the store got wilder and wilder. Time was running out and the shoppers were getting desperate. They plowed through Hope's carefully arranged displays like a heard of stampeding cattle, they snapped at her if she was too slow waiting on them, and it took all of Hope's control to keep from snapping back.

Mrs. Randolph didn't make things any easier. Once, during a rare period of calm, Hope had jokingly suggested that they mark the prices up so high all the customers would leave. But her boss was not amused. She actually thought Hope was serious, and for the rest of the day, she kept checking the price tags to make sure they hadn't been changed.

"Hope?" Her little brother, James, was looking at her. "Can we play Scrabble tonight?"

"Not tonight," Hope said. "I've got a date, remember?"

James, who hadn't discovered girls yet, made a face. "Well, how about tomorrow night?"

Hope shook her head. "I'm sorry, James, I'll be working tomorrow night."

Mrs. Chang's fork of broccoli stopped halfway to her mouth. "At night, Hope? I thought you got off at four-thirty."

"Usually I do," Hope told her. "But another girl quit and since Christmas is only four days away, things are really busy. So they asked me to work a few extra hours."

"I hope this doesn't mean you'll be working late on Christmas Eve," Dr. Chang said.

"I'm sure they'll hire somebody by then," Hope said, mentally crossing her fingers. "But even if they don't, I'd only be working until seven-thirty."

"Seven-thirty!" James broke in. "You can't do that! You'd miss the tree-trimming and everything!"

Trimming the tree together on Christmas Eve was a tradition in the Chang family. While they decorated it with delicate glass balls and handmade ornaments, they munched on pizza and popcorn, washing them down with cider, and then Hope played carols on the piano. It was Hope's favorite part of the holiday, and she couldn't imagine Christmas without it.

"I haven't been scheduled to work then," she said again. "But if I am, I'll only be a little late. And anyway, I couldn't just refuse to work. I've got a responsibility."

Hope was sure that would take care of any arguments. After all, it was her parents who had taught her about the importance of responsibility.

But Dr. Chang didn't seem impressed by Hope's sense of obligation this time. After exchanging glances with his wife, he turned to Hope. "You have a responsibility to your family, too, you realize. But more important, Hope, you have one to yourself."

"I don't understand."

"We worry that you're not happy," Mrs. Chang said. "We know you love your music, but you haven't played a note since vacation started. You don't have time for us, and you don't have time for yourself, for the things you really like to do. And what about Peter? You haven't had much time for him, either, and I'm sure neither of you is happy about that."

"I see Peter every day at cheerleading practice," Hope reminded her. "And I'm going out with him tonight. Mother, Father," she went on, "everything is fine, really." If she'd been another person, Hope might have said, "will you stop bugging me?" But Hope Chang couldn't say that to her parents. Instead, she politely asked if she could be excused, cleared the dinner dishes, and went upstairs to shower.

When Peter arrived at seven-thirty, Hope was still in her room, getting dressed. Hoping he didn't look as nervous as he felt, Peter followed Dr. and Mrs. Chang into the living room and sat down to wait.

"Are you having a good vacation, Peter?" Dr. Chang asked.

"Fine, thanks. It's nice to have a break from school."

"I'm sure it is," Mrs. Chang said. "How is the new cheerleader coming along? Hope hasn't said much about him."

"Well, we've only had three workouts with him, so it's still kind of rough." Rough was putting it mildly, Peter thought. But if he said any more, he'd have to start answering a bunch of questions about why Rob was on the squad, and he didn't want to get into that.

He glanced around the room, trying to find something to talk about. Over by the baby grand piano was the still-undecorated Christmas tree. It was tall and full, and he could smell the fresh pine from where he sat. A lot different from the artificial tabletop model his mother brought out of storage every year.

On the piano's music stand was some sheet music. To Peter the black notes looked incredibly complicated. "I see Hope's been playing," he remarked. "I'm glad she found the time — I know she loves it."

Dr. and Mrs. Chang exchanged amused glances. "To tell you the truth, I'm the one who's been playing," Mrs. Chang said to Peter. "Hope's job keeps her too busy. But you're right about her loving music."

"I wish she hadn't taken that job," Peter blurted out. He hadn't meant to say it at all, but now that he had, he felt he had to explain himself. "I . . . I mean . . ." he stammered, "not that there's anything wrong with working in a department store over vacation, but I can't believe Hope likes it. I think she'd be happier doing the things she loves while she has the chance."

Before the Changs could answer, Hope walked into the living room. She was wearing gray wool pants and a cranberry-colored sweater that looked beautiful with her gleaming dark hair. Her eyes were bright, her cheeks were flushed, and most people would have thought she was excited about going to a party.

Not Peter. Peter knew her better than most people, and what Peter saw in her face was not the flush of excitement. Hope had obviously overheard what he'd said to her parents, and her face was red because she was angry. Angry at him.

Settling back on Sean's deep leather couch, Pres Tilford popped a cheese curl into his mouth and grinned at Patrick. "Is it my imagination, or do I sense a lot of tension in the air?"

"You'd have to be dead to miss it," Patrick replied. "Sorry, I just can't relax. Not after what happened today. And I shouldn't have let you talk me into coming, either. I guess I didn't think she'd be here."

"Well, she is." Pres looked at Jessica. She was across the room, talking to two boys from the basketball team, who couldn't seem to take their eyes off her. No wonder, Pres thought, grinning again. She's a knockout anytime, but in that silky green blouse, she's downright dangerous.

"Actually, I would have been surprised if she hadn't shown up," he said to Patrick. "She's too proud to hole up in her room just because you two had a fight. Besides, I told you, you'll work it out. You're perfect for each other. Just consider this a pothole in the road to nirvana."

"Some pothole," Patrick commented, but he couldn't help laughing.

"Anyway," Pres went on, "I don't think you're the only one who's uptight."

"Oh? Who else is?"

"That I don't know." Pres took a sip of his soda and stood up. "But I think I'll take a stroll and see if I can find out."

Pres was right about the tension in the air, but on the surface, everything seemed to be going great. The Dubrow's large living room looked spectacular: A gigantic tree decorated with blinking blue lights and tiny glass balls stood in front of the bay window; a long table covered with a holiday cloth held bowls and platters of enough food to feed an army; and because of the candles Sean had bought that afternoon, the room smelled of bayberry and pine.

"Hey, great party, Sean," Pres said. "Nice sweater, too."

"Thanks." Sean glanced down at his burgundy wool sweater — recently bought at Langston's, thanks to Hope — and for a moment, his spirits lifted. But not very high. "Well, listen," he said to Pres, "help yourself to the food, or find somebody to dance with." He gestured toward the dining room, which had been cleared for dancing. "I gotta make sure everybody's happy."

Nodding, Pres made his way over to Olivia

and David, and once they started talking, Sean moved across the room. On the outside, he was his usual smooth self, smiling and joking with everyone. But inside, he was feeling very edgy. Things were not going exactly as he'd planned.

He'd hung the mistletoe — three bunches of it — just as he'd promised Tara. But as far as he was concerned, it was being completely wasted. He thought that he and Lisa were dates as well as co-hosts. That seemed logical. This whole party had been Lisa's idea, and when they'd planned it three weeks ago, she'd obviously been hoping that the two of them might get something steady going.

But tonight, Lisa seemed about as thrilled to be with Sean as with a brother. Ever since she'd shown up, she'd hardly said two words to him. She didn't act angry; she just didn't act interested. And unfortunately, Sean knew why. He'd seen the look on her face that morning, watching Rob Ladd pretend to be a cheerleader. She looked like most girls looked when they saw their favorite rock star — in a trance.

Sean wasn't really heartbroken over Lisa's defection. There were plenty of other girls around. It was the principle of the thing that was bothering him. And Tara hadn't arrived yet, either. That was beginning to bug him. Was she ticked off about Lisa that she wasn't even going to show?

Things weren't going right, and even though Sean put up a good front, he kept trying to figure out how to turn everything around to his advantage. His mind wasn't really on his party, and Pres had picked up on it.

"Looks like our host has something heavy on his mind," Pres commented to Olivia and David.

"Mmm." Olivia wasn't particularly interested in Sean's problem at the moment. She had her own to deal with.

"Well, listen," Pres said, ignoring her bad mood, "when's somebody going to tell me about Rob Ladd? Did Mrs. Engborg ever explain why he's on the team?"

"Oh, not you, too!" Olivia remarked. "Can't you come up with a more interesting topic of conversation?"

"It's my fault, Pres," David said cheerfully. "According to Livvy, I've been badgering her about Ladd all night long."

"It happens to be true," Olivia said. "All you want to talk about is him."

"Sorry, but you know reporters. Curiosity is the nature of the beast." David turned to Pres. "For instance, just for argument's sake, let's say that Mrs. Engborg decided it would be a great idea to have seven cheerleaders instead of six."

"Okay."

"Well, doesn't it strike you as just a tiny bit funny that she picks a complete klutz for the job?"

"I have been wondering about that," Pres admitted with a grin.

"And then," David went on eagerly, "she starts changing the routines so that they're easy!"

"Not the coach's style at all," Pres agreed.

David was on the edge of his chair now, Olivia noticed glumly. He thought he was onto something big. Unfortunately, he was.

"I have an idea," David was saying, "that Robinson Ladd's bodyguard might know something."

"His bodyguard?"

"Sure, that guy I saw at practice the other day. The two of them were having a very intense discussion afterward."

Pres laughed. "That wasn't his bodyguard, Duffy. That was Judson Abbott."

"No kidding? The politician?" David's eyes widened. "Hey, Olivia, why didn't you tell me?"

"You didn't ask," Olivia pointed out.

"Wow, this makes things very interesting," David said. "There's definitely a story behind the story."

"Personally, I'm sick of the subject," Olivia remarked. She was crazy about David Duffy, but for once, she wished he'd stifle his curiosity. It was bad enough having Rob on the squad and having to keep the reason a secret. But on top of that, to have to listen to David's constant questions about it was too much. She wasn't cut out for this. Covering up, that's what she was doing, and it was starting to give her a stomachache.

Olivia took a sip of soda, hoping that would help. It didn't. Then she remembered that Angie Poletti, one of the old squad's cheerleaders, would be home from college in a day or two.

Olivia knew that if anybody could find a bright side to this situation, it would be Angie. That thought cheered her up, and she turned to David with a smile. "Look, let's make a deal. If you promise not to bug me about Rob Ladd anymore, I'll dance with you."

"There's something wrong with your reasoning," David said with a laugh. But he stood up and took Olivia's hand anyway. "Okay, let's dance."

Pres laughed, too, but before David and Olivia had danced more than two steps, he saw Olivia frown and head for the food table. Duffy had obviously broken the deal.

Shaking his head, Pres moved on, his eyes roving over the partyers. Hope Chang and Peter Rayman were standing in the archway to the dining room, and Pres headed for them, planning to suggest that they take advantage of the mistletoe hanging over their heads. As he got closer, he heard Peter say, "But I didn't tell them anything I haven't told you! I don't understand why you're so upset!"

Uh oh, Pres thought. More tension. Deciding to forget the joke about the mistletoe, he just smiled and said hi, then did a fast about-face.

Once she was sure that Pres wasn't going to join them, Hope turned back to Peter. "I'm upset because you joined sides with them," she said. She kept her voice low, but the anger in it couldn't be missed.

"Seems to me you ought to be glad," Peter told her. "I mean if your parents and I can see eye-to-eye on something, we ought to be celebrating, not fighting."

Hope ignored that remark. "You joined sides with them against me," she said. "Doesn't that explain why I'm angry?"

"No, because I'm not against you," Peter protested, "and neither are they. We're all on your side."

"You have a funny way of showing it." Hope took a deep breath. "Peter, listen, please. I'm sorry that you and my parents didn't want me to take this job — "

"It's not what *we* want," Peter broke in. "It's what *you* want."

"That doesn't make any sense! I wouldn't have taken it if I didn't want to!"

"I'm not so sure about that," Peter said, beginning to get angry himself. "I don't believe for a minute that you're happy snapping to attention for that drill sergeant of a boss. You just won't admit it."

"There's nothing to admit," Hope said quietly. "And there's no sense talking about it anymore, either." With that, she turned and headed into the living room, leaving a forlorn-looking Peter standing alone under the mistletoe.

Hope passed by Pres without saying a word, which was unusual. She was usually so friendly, so aware of everyone around her. But Pres noticed that her dark eyes were flashing, and he was glad he hadn't butted in on her conversation with Peter. With a shake of his head, he sat down next to Patrick, who still hadn't moved from his corner of the couch.

"Well?" Patrick asked, as if Pres had never left. "Who else is uptight?"

"Just about everybody," Pres reported. "I didn't talk to Jessica, but I figured she's probably in the same state you are."

"Doesn't look like it," Patrick said moodily. "She's been dancing with the same guy for twenty minutes."

"Don't let it get to you. She's crazy about you, any idiot could see it." Pres craned his neck and glanced around the crowded room. "I wonder where Tara Armstrong is?"

"Why? Are you interested in her?"

"No, not really. But she's a lot of fun. I figure she might lighten things up a little bit."

Sean was wondering exactly the same thing. Where was Tara? The party had been going on for an hour and she still hadn't shown up. Twice he'd gone to the phone to call her, and twice he'd changed his mind. Now, though, he decided to swallow his pride and see what was happening.

Sean was halfway to the kitchen when the doorbell rang. Lisa will get it, he thought, and kept on walking. Then he heard Lisa's voice, and what she said stopped him in his tracks.

"Tara!" Lisa cried. "We thought you'd never

get here. And Rob! Hi! I'm so glad you could make it!"

Wheeling around, Sean looked down the hall toward the front door. Framed in its arch like a picture stood Tara Armstrong. Next to her, his arm around her shoulder, stood Robinson Ladd.

CHAPTER

9

For a moment, Sean just stood there, trying to figure out what was going on. This was his house, right? His party. Was Robinson Ladd welcome here? No way. Tara was welcome, or at least she used to be. But now Sean wasn't so sure. Had she actually come with Rob Ladd, knowing how Sean felt about him?

"Come on in so I can close the door," Lisa was saying. "It's freezing out there!" Then, turning to Sean, who was standing as still as a zombie, she smiled. "I hope you don't mind, Sean. I invited Rob. I mean, all the other cheerleaders are here, why not him?"

Sean could have come up with a half-dozen good reasons not to invite Rob, but he decided not to go into them. Not right then, anyway. And much as he wanted to, he decided he couldn't kick the guy out, either. It just wouldn't be cool.

Giving himself a mental shake, Sean flashed a cocky grin and walked over to Rob. "Why don't you take off your coat and stay awhile?" he said, trying to sound sincere. "There's plenty of food."

Rob raised an eyebrow. It was obvious, to him anyway, that Sean hadn't meant a word he'd just said. "But is there plenty of fun? That's the question," he said with a smile.

Lisa laughed and tugged at his coat sleeve. "Of course there's plenty of fun," she cooed. "Would I give a party that wasn't fun?"

So it's *her* party now, Sean thought. Gritting his teeth to keep back all the sarcastic remarks that were threatening to come out, he watched as Rob Ladd took off his jacket. It was a half length pea coat, and it had to be at least ten years old, its navy wool threadbare at the cuffs and collar. But underneath, Ladd was wearing a great-looking hand-woven fisherman's sweater. Imported for sure, Sean thought. Probably cost a fortune.

Sean was beginning to get an idea of Rob Ladd's style. Contrast was the key. Like the worn-out jacket over the imported sweater. Or the frayed and holey sweat suit with the five-hundred-dollar gold watch. Something to show he was just folks, plus something to remind the folks that he was really a notch above them.

Sean didn't like the style at all, but the girls obviously did. Three more Ladd groupies had joined Lisa now, and they were all competing for the golden boy's attention.

Disgusted and frustrated, Sean turned away and came face-to-face with Tara, who had just finished taking off her coat. She wore lavender crushed-velvet pants, a creamy silk blouse, and a silver necklace around her slender throat. She was one of the best-looking girls at the party, but for once, Sean was immune to her charms. Without a word, he turned his back on her and walked away.

What's eating him? Tara wondered as she reached up to fluff her hair. He acts like I'm contagious. Then she caught sight of the rest of the cheerleaders in the living room. Olivia, Jessica, Peter, and Hope were all staring at her so hard she felt like she was on trial.

"What's the matter?" she asked, moving into the living room. "Are my pants ripped? Is there a disgusting stain on the front of my blouse?"

Olivia came right to the point. "I don't know about anybody else, but I was wondering how you could possibly show up at this party with Rob Ladd."

"What do you mean?"

"Tara," Jessica said, "how could you be his date? Rob Ladd, of all people?"

"I'm not his date," Tara told them. "I was late because my father's car had a flat, would you believe it? And when I finally got here, Rob was just pulling up. We came to the door together, that's all."

"Oh. Sorry," Olivia said. "What's he doing here, anyway?"

"Lisa invited him," Tara reported. "And Sean is ready to explode." Now she knew why Sean had treated her like the invisible woman — he thought she was Rob's date, too.

Glancing around for somebody to dance with, Tara spotted Sean slouched against the door frame, looking extremely grumpy. You'd better explain the situation to him, too, she told herself, not that he really deserves an explanation.

But when she got close, Sean reached out a hand and caught her arm in a tight grip. "I knew you liked to play tricks," he said softly, so no one else could hear, "but I didn't think you liked to play dirty."

"If you're talking about the fact that I came to the door with Rob," Tara said, prying his fingers from her arm, "that's all I did. I came to the door with him, not to the party. We just happened to get here at the same time."

"Wasn't that convenient?" he said sarcastically.

"Well, if you don't believe me, why don't you ask him?" With a nod of her head, Tara indicated Rob, who was over by the food table, surrounded by girls. Including Lisa Hutton, Tara noticed with satisfaction. After a moment, Rob seemed to sense that he was being watched. He turned his head, saw Tara looking at him, and smiled as if they were the only two people in the room. Then he stepped free from the circle of admiring girls and went over to Tara and Sean.

"Hey, Dubrow, you throw a good party," he said, never taking his eyes off Tara.

"Thanks."

Draping an arm around Tara's shoulder, Rob asked, "You don't mind if I take your girl away from you, I hope. I'd like to dance, and I've heard she's one of the best."

* * *

"You're the best,
Don't let it slide!
Tell that team. . . ."

With a clap of her hands, Ardith Engborg brought the cheer to a stop. "Start again," she said. "And try to breathe a little life into it this time."

"You're the best,
Don't let it slide!
Tell that team,
To step aside!"

"Hold it, hold it!" the coach yelled. Everyone stopped again, and Mrs. Engborg shook her head in disgust. "You've been trudging through those steps like your shoes have cement in them. You move like you're walking in your sleep. I know there was a party last night, but I didn't think it was going to last till morning."

Six of the cheerleaders — the "old-timers" — looked guiltily at the floor. They hadn't stayed up partying all night, but they knew they weren't performing well. All the tensions and arguments had caught up with them this morning, and none of them could keep their minds on cheerleading.

Only Rob Ladd looked cheerful and guilt-free. "I have a feeling, Mrs. Engborg, that holiday fever has struck."

Sean waited hopefully for the coach to cut Rob down with a withering remark. Nobody could make a lame excuse like that and get away with it.

But the coach's reply, much to Sean's disappointment, was extremely tame. "I know Christmas is only three days away," she said, "but we've got work to do. So let's try to keep our minds on it."

With a collective sigh, the cheerleaders got in position again.

"You're on top,
So don't slow down!
Run that team,
Right out of town!"

This was already one of their easiest cheers. There were no daring gymnastic moves, no handsprings or lifts or pyramids. The only real zip came at the end, with the boys doing stag leaps as the girls did the splits. And having Rob Ladd wouldn't have changed it much at all, except that he couldn't do a stag leap.

That wasn't quite true, Olivia told herself. He could do a stag leap. It was just that Sean and Peter's leaps took them three feet into the air, while Rob managed to propel himself only inches off the ground.

They tried it two more times, and then Mrs. Engborg signaled them to stop. "Let's cut the stag leaps," she said. "We'll keep the splits, but I want you boys to space yourselves in a line behind the girls and strike a pose." She stood up, legs wide apart, fists bunched on her hips. "Like this. And don't forget to smile."

Peter stepped forward. "But Mrs. Engborg, that's going to change the whole look of it." He spoke quietly, but five of the cheerleaders could tell he was upset.

"I agree," Jessica spoke up. "It's going to look funny with the guys just standing there."

"Let me be the judge of that, please," Mrs. Engborg told them. "Let's try it."

They tried it.

"It looks fine," the coach said. "Okay, I have to make a call in my office. Olivia, you take them through it again."

As Mrs. Engborg left the gym, all eyes turned to Olivia, who felt her stomach twist. Wasn't it enough that Rob Ladd was on the squad, and that she had to keep the reason a secret, especially from David? Did she have to help the guy ruin one of their cheers?

104

That's what you said you'd do, she reminded herself, as she caught Jessica's green eyes watching her. You said that keeping the squad together was the most important thing. And you're the captain, so you'd better do it, because nobody else will.

Her stomach hurting a little bit more with each step, Olivia got into position for the cheer. "Okay," she said, looking everybody in the eye, "let's get going. Let's see if we can have this nailed down before the coach comes back."

By the time practice was over, the pain in Olivia's stomach had eased up. Rob, thank goodness, was able to stand with his hands on his hips and smile, so the routine had gone okay.

As she pulled on her yellow knit hat and stepped outside into a bitter cold wind, Olivia tried not to think about the fact that their routines were getting simpler by the minute. Any more changes like getting rid of stag leaps, and they might as well just stand in a line and shout, Rah, rah!

Olivia stuffed her hands in her pockets, bent her head, and began walking home at a brisk pace, trying to keep warm. Having just a simple, rah-rah squad would be better than having no squad at all, she thought. She knew Jessica didn't agree with her. Jessica had performed the routine with about as much gusto as a robot, and Peter wasn't much better. Hope and Tara had worked hard, and Sean had surprised Olivia with his energy. But she knew he couldn't stand the sight of Rob Ladd, so maybe his energy was mostly anger. She hoped he would manage to keep a lid on it, or there might be trouble. Things were bad enough — a knock-down, drag-out fight between Rob and Sean would just about finish everything.

Stop thinking like that, she told herself, feeling her stomach tighten up again. It's that kind of thinking that can lead to an ulcer.

Turning the corner onto her street, Olivia was hit by a gust of wind so strong that it pushed her sideways. Off balance, she stepped out with one foot and hit a smooth, glassy patch of ice. Her foot flew up into the air, and just like a cartoon character, she landed hard, right on her backside.

Nice move, Olivia, she told herself. I can see David's headline now: GYMNASTIC WHIZ GOES WHOOPS! Picking herself up off the freezing sidewalk, she limped toward home. She thought the limp would be gone by the time she got to her house, but it wasn't. Maybe you can use this, she thought. It would give David something to write about and it might take his mind off Rob Ladd.

No one else was home, and Olivia figured her mother was out shopping. Good. That would give her a chance to soak the soreness out in a hot bath. If her mother saw her limping, she'd hustle her off to bed and call the doctor.

Olivia took off her jacket and boots, got some apple juice from the refrigerator, and was just about ready to leave the kitchen when she saw the note by the telephone. Angie Poletti had called. She was home from college and would Olivia call back as soon as possible. (But don't tie up the phone all afternoon, Mrs. Evans had added.)

Eager to talk to Angie, Olivia was just reaching for the phone when it rang. It was David Duffy.

"Any late-breaking news on the Rob Ladd mystery?" he asked.

"You have a one-track mind," Olivia said.

"Not true at all," David protested.

"Oh, really? Tell me something else you're thinking about besides Rob."

"I'm sitting here wondering what you gave me for Christmas," he told her. "It looks like a shoe box, but you wouldn't give me a pair of shoes, would you? Not that I couldn't use them."

"I might." Olivia had given him her present the night before, and the hat *was* in a shoe box. Maybe she should have given him shoes. He sure didn't need a Sherlock Holmes hat. "You'll just have to wait until Sunday to find out," she said. "What are you doing at home, anyway?"

"Getting ready to go out again," David said. "I just talked to my boss at the paper, and he wants me to follow up on the Ladd thing."

"What do you mean, 'follow up'?"

"Find out the real reason he's on the squad."

Olivia's stomach immediately went into its

knot-tying act. "I just don't understand why you're doing this."

"Because it's my job, for one thing," David explained.

"It is not! You're not an investigative reporter," Olivia retorted. "Why can't you just drop this subject?"

"Maybe because you keep telling me to," David shot back. "Methinks the lady doth protest too much."

Olivia took a deep breath. Of course she'd been protesting too much. She wasn't used to covering up the truth, especially with David. More than anything, she wanted to tell him what was going on with the squad. But if she did, she might ruin everything. But if she didn't, and David found out, anyway, she might ruin *them*. With that thought, her stomach twisted itself into a second knot.

"Okay, David," she said quietly. "Go ahead and follow up on your story. But please, don't ask me any more questions about it. Please?"

"Gee, my main source just clammed up on me." David laughed, but Olivia could tell he was confused and hurt. "Well, all right, Livvy," he went on. "I'll call you later, okay?"

"Okay. 'Bye, David." Olivia hung up, then immediately lifted the receiver again and started dialing Angie's number. After that conversation, she needed Angie's bright, cheerful attitude more than ever. Before she finished dialing, though, the doorbell rang.

Olivia hung up, and still limping, went to the front door. Maybe it was a Christmas package from her father's parents. Or a Christmas package from her mother's parents. Or the meter reader. She opened the door.

It was Walt Manners.

CHAPTER

Walt Manners, Olivia's first and former boyfriend, didn't wait for her reaction. With a big grin, he reached down, swooped her up, and gave her a breath-squeezing bear hug. "Olivia Evans!" he cried, holding her so that for once, she was as tall as he was. "My, how you've grown!"

"Walt!" Olivia could hardly believe it was him, but there was no mistaking this husky, good-natured guy for anyone else. "Put me down, come in out of the cold, and then tell me what you're doing in Tarenton!"

Laughing, Walt set her back on her feet and stepped inside. "Thought you'd seen the last of me, I'll bet."

"Not really, but I sure didn't expect to see you now. I thought you'd be in New York." Walt's parents had moved to the Big Apple during the past summer, and Walt had transferred to college there just a few months before. Leading him into the kitchen, Olivia poured him some of her apple juice. "Are you going to tell me what you're doing here, or do I have to guess?"

"It's no mystery — " Walt began.

"Good," Olivia interrupted. "The last thing I need is a mystery."

"My folks sold the house," Walt went on. "And there's still a lot of stuff stashed in it, so I volunteered to come out and do some packing. I'm staying with my aunt and uncle, and I'll be here through Christmas." Walt lounged in one of the kitchen chairs and drank some juice. "So. What's happening in little old Tarenton?"

"Oh, you know, the usual things," Olivia said, trying to decide whether to tell him about Rob Ladd. Might as well get it over with, she thought, he'll find out from Pres anyway. "We . . . uh . . . the squad's looking good. We have a seventh cheerleader now. Another boy. Robinson Ladd."

"The senator's son?"

"Yes, did you know him?"

Walt shook his head. "Only by sight. How's he working out?"

"Not very well. Not yet, anyway."

"Oh." Walt shrugged and drank some more. "Well, Ardith'll whip him into shape, that's for sure. What else is happening?"

Olivia couldn't believe it. No questions about

111

why Rob was on the squad, or what Mrs. Engborg thought she was doing? Wasn't Walt the least bit curious?

Obviously he wasn't. He was sitting there waiting for her to tell him what else was happening. Olivia shook her head in relief. It felt so great not having to answer a bunch of questions that she laughed.

"What's so funny?" Walt wanted to know.

"Nothing." Olivia laughed again. "Oh. Angie's back. I was just calling her when you came to the door. Want me to call her now? Maybe the three of us can go get some pizza or something."

"Sounds great, but I can't right now," Walt said. "I have to get out to the house. The real estate agent said something about checking the pipes to make sure they don't freeze. Hey!" He leaped up from the chair. "If you're not busy, why don't you come with me? We can call Angie when we get back and maybe get together then."

"Well, I. . . . Okay!" There was no reason not to go, Olivia thought, reaching for her coat and boots. She scribbled a note to her mother and turned to Walt, smiling. "Let's go!"

On the drive out to Walt's house — a log and glass structure in the woods, from which his parents had hosted a morning television talk show — he brought Olivia up to date on all his news. He made her laugh with stories about getting lost on the New York subways. He told her about college and how he still wasn't sure what he wanted to major in. He brought greetings from Mary Ellen

Kirkwood, who was in New York trying to become a model, and couldn't get home to Tarenton for the holidays because she'd finally landed a job that could lead to something big.

"Nancy Goldstein won't be here, either," Olivia said, mentioning another cheerleader from the old squad. "Her family's going to Florida."

"So it's just you and me and Angie and Pres, huh? I've got an idea," Walt said. "Why don't the four of us get together tonight?"

"That sounds great." Olivia smiled as she thought of it — four "old-timers" reminiscing together. Still smiling, she glanced at Walt. He was so easy to be with. He never seemed to be down or uptight, and he never took anything too seriously. That used to bother Olivia sometimes. She'd wondered if he planned to spend the rest of his life clowning around.

Today, though, it didn't bother her a bit. For the first time in days, she found that she was completely relaxed. Her stomach didn't hurt, she wasn't tempted to chew her fingernails, and by the time they'd reached Walt's house, she realized that she hadn't had a single thought about Rob Ladd, the troubles on the squad, or David Duffy's questions.

Angie Poletti brushed her blonde hair back from her shining face, took a sip of her chocolate milkshake, and leaned forward. "Now," she said eagerly, "I want to hear everything about David Duffy."

113

Olivia looked over at Walt, who was standing at the counter in Freddy's Diner, waiting for an order of French fries. The three of them (Pres had a date and couldn't make it) had come there after dinner, and since Walt was out of earshot, there was no reason for her not to discuss David. Except that she just didn't feel like it. "There's not really much to say," she told Angie. "He's a freshman in college, he has a part-time job with the newspaper, and he's . . . nice."

"Nice!" Angie laughed. "I hope so. But Livvy, what color's his hair? What color are his eyes? What's his personality like? Come on, I'm dying to know!"

"Blond hair, blue eyes."

"And?" Angie urged. "Olivia! I thought you were madly in love with him!"

Olivia shifted uncomfortably. "Well, I don't know about 'madly,'" she said. "I mean, I care about him. But 'madly in love'? That's pretty strong."

"Oh." Angie looked confused for a moment, but then she brightened up. "I guess that explains why you're here with Walt tonight instead of out with David."

"Well, Walt's only going to be here for a few days," Olivia explained, "so I wanted to see as much of him as I could. They sold their house, you know, and once the new people have moved in, Walt might never have any reason to come back to Tarenton."

"I will always come back to Tarenton," Walt said, scooting into the booth beside Olivia. "How could I stay away when you two are here?"

"Who says we'll always be here?" Angie asked, helping herself to one of his French fries.

"My crystal ball," Walt said, staring into his empty Coke glass. "It tells me that Angie will open a school for disadvantaged kids, and Olivia will someday replace Ardith Engborg as the terror of the Tarenton High Varsity Squad."

Angie and Olivia burst into laughter, and for the rest of the evening, Olivia felt the way she had with Walt earlier that day — relaxed, free, and totally unworried.

The good feeling even carried over into next morning's cheerleading practice. For the first time, the sight of Rob Ladd fumbling a supremely simple move didn't make Olivia cringe. Things would work out, she was sure of it, and besides, this was the last practice until after Christmas. She wouldn't have to look at Rob Ladd or think about cheerleading for three whole days.

It wasn't until the squad took a break and Olivia was sitting on one of the lower bleachers, drinking some water, that she realized things weren't quite as rosy as she'd thought.

"I guess we sort of got our wires crossed yesterday." David Duffy had suddenly and silently appeared at Olivia's side. His eyes were almost the exact shade of blue as his sweater. "I called you

115

last night, but your mother said you'd gone out. Were we going to get together, or was that just my overactive imagination?"

Olivia gulped down some water, suddenly feeling guilty. "Well, we didn't really decide whether we were going to do anything," she said, "but you did say you were going to call. I'm sorry," she went on, feeling her cheeks get warm with shame, "I completely forgot."

"Well, hey, don't get all racked up about it." Casually, David reached up and tucked a strand of hair behind her ear. "I just wanted to make sure I hadn't goofed up. I didn't mean to put you on the spot."

Olivia, feeling very conscious of the spot she was in, smiled. "No, you didn't goof up. I did."

"Okay." David nodded. "Now that we've figured out who's guilty, how about this afternoon? Want to catch a movie? You've got your choice between two Christmas specials, both guaranteed to smother you in sweetness."

Olivia laughed, but her feelings took a turn for the worse. She and Walt were going ice-skating that afternoon. "I wish I could," she said, "but . . . David, this old friend is in town and we made plans for this afternoon."

"Oh, yeah? That's nice. Who is it? Mary Ellen?" David knew the old squad by name, if not by sight.

"No, she's still in New York."

"Nancy?"

Olivia shook her head. "She's in Florida." She was tempted to tell him it was Angie, but with her luck, the story would backfire. Besides, she'd already done enough covering up with David. "It's Walt Manners," she said, speaking quickly to get it over with. "He's in town for just a few days and it might be a long time before I ever see him again."

David nodded again. He knew all about Walt Manners. A friendly, well-liked guy who used to be on the Tarenton High Varsity Squad. He also used to be Olivia Evans' boyfriend. "Well," he said, pulling out his blue knit sailor's cap, "I'll bet you cut a fabulous figure eight. Just don't break a leg, Livvy, the squad needs you." With a dimpled grin, he stood up and strolled out of the gym.

Olivia watched him go, wishing he had never shown up at all. If he hadn't, he would never have found out about Walt. And if he hadn't found out about Walt, then she would never have seen the hurt in his brilliant blue eyes.

"Hey, everybody!" Rob Ladd broke in on Olivia's thoughts. "Before we get back to work, I have an announcement to make."

The other cheerleaders looked at him, everyone except Tara hoping that maybe he'd decided to quit the squad. No such luck, though.

"The Ladd family is holding its traditional holiday open house on December twenty-eighth. It's a late-afternoon buffet, beginning around three o'clock. I'm afraid it won't come close to rivaling

117

the kind of party Dubrow throws," Rob said, giving a nod to Sean, "but we aim to please. Anyway, you're all invited."

No one had been expecting the invitation, and they greeted it in silence.

Smiling, Rob went on. "I hate to seem pushy, but I'm at the mercy of the caterers. They insist on having some idea of exactly how many mouths they'll be feeding. So maybe you can tell me now whether you can make it or not."

Tara, who wouldn't have missed a buffet at the Ladd house if her life depended on it, nodded quickly. "I'll be there, Rob," she said with a charming smile. "I'm sure it'll be wonderful."

Hope, who would be working the afternoon of the twenty-eighth, was the only one with a legitimate excuse, and even though she was secretly glad she didn't have to go, only Peter suspected that she wasn't sincerely sorry about it.

But the rest of the cheerleaders, caught by surprise, didn't have time to come up with reasons why they couldn't attend the late-afternoon buffet, especially not with Rob staring them in the eyes, waiting for an answer.

One by one, Peter, Jessica, and Olivia nodded. They nodded reluctantly, but Rob didn't seem to notice. Turning to Sean, he coolly raised an eyebrow. "Dubrow? Can we look forward to your presence? Or will we have to make do without it?"

Still smarting from the way Rob had taunted him at his own party, Sean gazed at the ceiling, trying to decide what to do. It was on the tip of his tongue to say something like, Sorry, Ladd, but I prefer love in the late afternoon, not food.

Then Sean saw that Tara was looking at him. Well? her eyes seemed to say. He's challenging you. Are you going to accept or turn tail and run?

Straightening his shoulders, Sean matched Rob grin for grin. "Sure. I'll be there, Ladd," he said. "Count on it."

CHAPTER

11

Later that afternoon, Sean started to have doubts about what he'd done. He knew Ladd was out to get him one way or another, and he wasn't sure that going to the party was such a good idea after all. Maybe it would have been smarter just to keep cool and stay away. Let Tara and the other Ladd groupies drool over the senator's son. Sean didn't need them. He didn't even want them, not if they had the bad taste to fall for Robinson Ladd.

On the other hand, Sean thought, if he canceled now, Ladd would really have something to hold over his head. And the last thing Sean wanted was to give ammunition to his enemy. If Sean backed out of going to the party, Ladd would find a way to needle him with it, over and over and over again.

It was five-thirty and it was already dark outside. Sean plugged in the Christmas tree cord, stretched out on the long leather couch, and stared at the blinking lights.

It didn't happen often, but this was one of the times when he wished he had someone to talk to. Tara was one of the few people who came to mind, but now, with her being so struck with Ladd fever, Sean knew it wouldn't work out.

He considered Peter Rayman. The two of them had become almost friends since they'd discovered a mutual dislike of Rob Ladd. But almost friends wasn't quite good enough. Besides, Sean couldn't see himself letting Rayman in on how insecure he felt.

Tara and Peter. Was that it? Sean sat up on the couch and ran through a mental list of people's names. Olivia and Jessica were out — he didn't feel that comfortable with them. Lisa was out — she was in Ladd's court. Pres Tilford — Sean had never really gotten to know the guy. Yes — Tara and Peter, that was it.

"Hey, ho!" Sean's father, his dark hair dusted with a light coat of snow, stuck his head around the living room door. "What's with the dark? Got a girl with you?"

Sean sat up and arranged a smile on his face. "You know me better than that, Dad. I'd have warned you first."

Mark Dubrow laughed and unzipped his overcoat. "Right. So, why are you sitting there with only the tree for company?"

121

"No reason," Sean said with a shrug. "I like to watch blinking lights, I guess."

"Hey." Sean's father walked over to the couch and peered down at his son. "You okay?"

"Sure. Well, a little tired, maybe."

"Boy, I know that feeling!" Mark Dubrow took off his sports coat, loosened his tie, and rolled up his sleeves. "Some of the characters you have to deal with out there in the business world. . . ." He shook his head and whistled softly. "It can really get dirty, let me tell you."

"I'll bet," Sean said, thinking of a certain character he had to deal with in the school world. "What happened?"

"Come on, let's go see what Windy left us to eat, and I'll tell you."

In the refrigerator, they found meatloaf and a salad. Sean stuck the meat in the microwave and set out some plates, while his father sliced a loaf of French bread and poured milk.

"I had an appointment this afternoon," Mark Dubrow said. "A very important customer, someone I've been trying to land for months. In fact, this was the first time he even agreed to see me."

"What went wrong?" Sean asked, as they sat down to eat.

His father drank some milk and shook his head. "You wouldn't believe it. I get there ten minutes early, I've got my sales pitch all ready — why Tarenton Fabricators can't be beat, why we've got the best reputation in three states, all backed up with statistics, right?"

Sean took a slice of meatloaf and nodded.

"So there I am, in the reception area, waiting, and who comes out of the guy's office? A salesman for Romax," Mark Dubrow said, mentioning Tarenton Fabricators' strongest competitor. "It turns out this Romax salesman has been bad-mouthing my company all along, and if I hadn't been there, ready to set everything straight, I probably would have lost the deal!"

"But you got it, right?"

"Sure, I got it!" Sean's father laughed and then shook his head again. "But talk about playing dirty! Can you believe that Romax guy?"

Sean could believe him, all right. He knew someone who played just as dirty. In a way it was different, of course — his father was dealing in the business world, and Sean was trying to make his way in school. But, still, they were both up against people who went behind their backs, who tried to ruin their reputations, who didn't care what they did or who they hurt, just as long as they came out on top.

"Today, I was just plain lucky," Sean's father was saying.

"It wasn't all luck," Sean pointed out. "You were prepared for the meeting, like you said. If you hadn't been, your customer might have gone with Romax."

"You know, you're right." Mark Dubrow smiled and lifted his milk glass in a toast. "Here's to being prepared. Guess my Boy Scout days weren't a total waste!"

123

After they ate, Sean's father hurried to take a shower — he had a date — and while Sean cleaned up the kitchen, he thought about being prepared. Or, in his case, *not* being prepared. That's why Rob Ladd had been able to get his goat so often. He kept catching Sean by surprise. From now on, Sean told himself, don't let anything that guy does surprise you. Just expect the worst and you'll be prepared, too.

He felt good now, and feeling good always made him want to do something. No sense sitting around the house when he could be sitting in his Fiero, going somewhere. After telling his father he was going out, Sean pulled on his down jacket, got in his car, and headed for Freddy's Diner. There was always some action at Freddy's and when his spirits were high, Sean wanted action.

Freddy's was crowded, just as Sean expected it to be, and when he walked in, several girls turned and called out greetings to him. Sean felt his spirits soar even higher. There was nothing like having a girl's eyes light up the minute she saw you to make you feel like a million bucks.

Waving casually, Sean scanned the rest of the crowd, trying to decide which table to join. That was when he spotted a cascade of flaming red curls belonging to a girl in one of the back tables. He couldn't see her face, but he didn't need to. Only one girl had hair that color — Tara Armstrong.

Maybe now's your chance to get everything straight with her, Sean thought. Putting on his best grin, he started making his way through the crowded tables. Fortunately, he saw who Tara was sitting with before he reached her. It was Robinson Ladd.

He got you again, Dubrow, Sean told himself as he whirled around and headed toward the front of the diner. What happened to being prepared? And why are you ducking out instead of facing the music?

Sean decided against ducking out, so he made himself welcome at one of the front tables, joining in the talk and laughter as if he were having the time of his life. But he wasn't quite ready to face the music, not yet, anyway. And the entire time he sat there, making jokes and conversation, the thought that kept running through his mind was, So she's dating him now.

Actually, it wasn't a date. Not officially. But no one at Freddy's knew that, and Tara wasn't about to set them straight. She had been out shopping, trying to find some stocking stuffers for her parents, and while she was shivering at the bus stop, who should drive by in his ancient, beat-up VW Bug, but Rob Ladd? And wasn't it a nice coincidence that they were both hungry, and that Freddy's was right across the street from the bus stop?

It had been wonderful, Tara thought, walking in and seeing so many heads turn in their direction. Girls wondering if Rob was off-limits now, and boys wondering the same thing about Tara.

Being the center of attention was Tara's favorite position, but she couldn't help feeling slightly relieved that none of the other cheerleaders was there to see her with Rob. They would definitely not approve. Privately, Tara thought it was about time they took their heads out of the sand and accepted the fact that Rob was on the squad to stay. But she wanted to keep that opinion to herself as long as she could.

Since Freddy's was cheerleader-free, though, Tara could relax and enjoy herself. This was the first time she'd ever been alone with Rob (if you could call sitting in a jam-packed diner being alone), and she planned to take advantage of it. She was determined to find out just who Rob Ladd was, and what made him tick. Right now, he was a big question mark, an unknown, and Tara was never comfortable with the unknown.

After they'd ordered cheeseburgers and Cokes, Tara shrugged off her deep purple jacket, twisted one of her red curls around a finger, and smiled across the table. "Tell me if I'm wrong, but I get the feeling you've never been here before."

Rob brushed a lock of brown hair off his forehead and laughed softly. "Your instinct is right on," he said. "I have never seen the inside of Freddy's Diner." Glancing around, he raised an eyebrow at the crowded room, the steamy windows, and the not-too-clean table. "This is the first time, and it just might be the last."

"Is there someplace else you'd rather go?"

126

Tara asked, wondering if he was really offended by the place. Was he used to high-class restaurants, or was he a snob?

"No, no, I was just kidding. Anyway, I'm not that familiar with any other place."

"Why not? Don't you ever go for pizza or hamburgers after school?"

"Almost never."

"Why not?" Tara asked again, wondering if this was another joke.

"Harvard."

"What?"

"Harvard." Rob smiled at her confusion. "My grandfather went there, my father went there, and now it's up to me to carry on the Ladd tradition. And Harvard frowns on people who stuff themselves with food after school instead of stuffing themselves with knowledge."

"In other words, you study a lot," Tara said.

"I couldn't have said it better myself."

Okay, Tara thought, he's not a snob, he just knows what he wants and what he has to do to get it. She liked that.

"But that's all over now," Rob said. "Not that I can afford to flunk out, but I've already applied. Now it's just a waiting game to see if all the work paid off."

Tara had a feeling it would. Rob Ladd seemed to have a way of getting what he wanted. "Are you going to follow your father's footsteps all the way and become a politician, too?"

There was that soft, almost soundless laugh again. "A good question," Rob told her. "The answer is yes. Do you want me to tell you why?"

"Sure," Tara said. "I mean, it's not a secret, is it?"

"Some politicians like to keep it quiet, so they cover it up by calling themselves public servants. But what they really love is the power." Rob leaned back and took a sip of his Coke. "I prefer being honest. I want the power, and if I can do some public good at the same time, so much the better."

"And if you can't?" Tara asked. "Do any good, I mean."

"Then I won't do any," he replied charmingly. "But I won't do any harm, either."

Their burgers arrived then, and for a few minutes they ate without talking. There was no doubt about it, Tara thought, Rob Ladd was one of the most intriguing boys she'd ever met. He wanted power, and he didn't mind admitting it. She also had no doubt that he'd get it. First Harvard, then law school, then some local election, and then what? Was she actually sitting here talking to a future president?

Suddenly, something occurred to her, and she laughed out loud.

"Want to let me in on the joke?" Rob asked.

"I was just thinking," Tara told me, "that it's a good thing you just got on the Varsity Squad. If you'd been on it for two years, you might never have had a chance to get into Harvard."

"Why's that?"

"Well, Mrs. Engborg can be a real slavedriver, haven't you noticed? Of course, everybody on the squad has to keep their grades up, but not high enough for Harvard."

"I think I'd have managed," Rob said quickly, without a trace of a smile, and Tara noticed that his eyes looked very hard. But the look was gone in a second, and Rob relaxed again. "To tell you the truth, I've been thinking a lot about the squad," he went on, leaning across the table and taking her hand.

"Oh?" This was the first time Rob had touched her, and Tara was very conscious of the cool, smooth feeling of his fingers. "What have you decided?"

"I really do think that all the routines would look better if there were only two boys instead of three," Rob said. "Seven's just not the right number of people; everything was smoother when there were six."

"Oh." Tara felt uncomfortable for the first time that night. She'd deliberately not talked about cheerleading, because she thought it might embarrass Rob. After all, he wasn't very good yet, and she didn't want to put herself in a position where she might have to praise him. She'd do it if he asked, but she hoped he wouldn't.

Besides, she thought, talk about even numbers. Rob's the odd man out. He forced his way onto the squad, and if anybody went, it would be him.

But Tara didn't want to think about how Rob got on the squad. It was too unpleasant, and besides, there was nothing anyone could do about it except try to make it work.

"Well," she said, "I'm sure Mrs. Engborg knows what she's doing. You'll see, by the time she's finished with us, the routines will look like they were written with seven people in mind."

Rob shook his head. "I still have my doubts, but. . . . Well, well," he said, glancing past her shoulder, "look who's here!"

Turning, Tara looked and saw the back of a tall, dark-haired boy moving toward the front of the restaurant. She knew plenty of dark-haired boys, but only one who walked like that, with so much confidence that he almost swaggered. It was Sean.

"It's Dubrow," Rob said. "Shall I invite him to join us?"

"No, don't," Tara said quickly. "I mean, we're just about finished and I have to go in a few minutes." Ordinarily, she would have welcomed the chance to see what happened when Rob and Sean came together. But Sean was still furious with her, and she was sure he'd use this against her by telling the other cheerleaders that he'd seen her out with the enemy. That, she wouldn't welcome.

"All right, we won't invite him. Now what were we talking about?" Rob said smoothly, still holding her hand. "Oh, right. Whether one of the guys should be eliminated from the Varsity Squad."

Tara heard him, but she didn't answer. She was still staring at the back of Sean's head, so she missed the triumphant look in Rob's pale blue eyes.

CHAPTER

 12

Saturday, December twenty-fourth. Peter sat at the kitchen table, picking at an extremely late breakfast of bacon and toast. He knew he should be feeling excited, or at least mellow — tomorrow was Christmas, after all — but instead he felt miserable.

It had been two days since Sean's party, two rotten days during which Hope had barely spoken to him. What did I do that was so wrong? he asked himself for the hundredth time. I told her parents I thought she'd be happier not working at a crowded department store. Her parents just happened to agree with me. But Hope sees it as some kind of conspiracy, like we're all ganging up on her. The result is misery.

"Peter, you've hardly touched your breakfast."

132

Peter's mother, Fran Rayman, came into the kitchen, searching through the pockets of her coat for the car keys. "You're not sick, I hope."

"No, I'm fine." Peter took a bite of bacon, chewing automatically. For all the appetite he had, it could have been cardboard.

"Are you sure?" Mrs. Rayman put a hand on his forehead, and Peter forced himself not to pull away. Since his parents' divorce, his mother had become super-protective. A sneeze might mean pneumonia, a cough could mean tuberculosis, and she didn't bother to hide the fact that she thought cheerleading was more dangerous than it needed to be. She worried that he didn't have enough friends, that he was too shy, and until he and Hope had gotten together, she'd pestered him about girls, too.

Peter knew that all her worrying meant she loved him, but sometimes he felt so stifled he actually had trouble breathing. Cheerleading was always a good escape, but he didn't have that today. Ice-skating with Hope would have been great, but that was definitely out.

Holding his half-eaten slice of bacon, Peter got up and wandered restlessly into the small living room. His mother had furnished it almost completely in wicker. She liked the summery look, she said. As a result, the small Christmas tree on the glass-topped wicker end table looked about as much at home as a palm tree in the mountains.

"It's nice, isn't it?" Mrs. Rayman asked, looking at the tree. She had followed him into the living room, buttoning her coat. "I sure am disappointed that I have to work today," she said with a sigh.

"Yeah, I don't blame you." His mother worked as a clerk in the hopsital, and she couldn't be choosy about her hours.

"Well, anyway, I'll be home after dinner, and we'll open our presents tonight. That way we can both sleep in tomorrow."

"Right, sounds great," Peter said, eyeing the pile of presents under the tree. It was a good thing he and Hope had exchanged gifts before their big blow up. He'd given her a bracelet, enameled in turquoise and rose, and edged with gold. He just hoped she wasn't so mad she'd throw it out.

"'Bye, sweetie, take care of yourself." Mrs. Rayman kissed Peter on the cheek and then hurried out the door.

After she'd left, Peter turned back to the tree, and in spite of everything that was on his mind, he couldn't help looking forward to finding out what was in some of those colorful packages. He really hoped his mother liked what he'd gotten her, but as he stared at the large box wrapped in red foil, he started to have doubts. It was an electric whirlpool-type bath for her feet, and when he'd bought it, he'd thought it was perfect. But the other day, when he'd told Sean about it, Sean had looked at him like he'd gone bonkers.

"You got her a what?" Sean had asked incredulously.

"Well, she's always complaining that her feet

are killing her by the end of the day," Peter had explained. "I thought she'd really appreciate it."

"Sure, but a footbath? For crying out loud, Rayman, it's not exactly . . . romantic."

"Sean, it's my mother we're talking about, not my girl friend," Peter argued.

"Hey, they're both women," Sean retorted. "And women like personal stuff, take my word for it. Do yourself and your mother a favor, why don't you. Spend an extra ten bucks and spring for something special — jewelry or perfume or something."

Deciding his mother deserved more than a footbath, Peter went into his bedroom, dressed, and checked his wallet and pants pockets. Seven dollars and some change. Back in the kitchen, he found four singles in the fruit bin of the refrigerator. His mother insisted on stashing money there, even though Peter kept telling her it was the first place a burglar would look.

Could he find something decent for eleven dollars and change? He could try. And he could try at Langston's.

Once inside the busy department store, Peter started to have doubts. Not about getting something nice for his mother; he found that right away — a pair of delicate earrings. They were totally impractical, and he hoped Sean was right about her liking something like this.

His doubts were about going to see Hope. That was the whole point of coming to Langston's, but now that he was there, he wasn't sure it was such a good idea. If they patched things up, it would be great, but they could just as easily have another argument. Things were shaky, but shaky was better than finished.

"Peter? I thought that was you."

Peter turned from the handbags he'd been staring at and found himself face-to-face with Hope's mother.

"Mrs. Chang, hi," Peter said. "It's nice to see you. It gives me a chance to wish you a Merry Christmas."

"Thank you, Peter, same to you." Mrs. Chang smiled warmly. "It looks like we're both doing some last-minute shopping."

Peter nodded, and then thought of something. "Mrs. Chang, I just bought a gift for my mother, and I wonder if you'd mind taking a look at it, to make sure it's okay."

Peter pulled out and opened the small box, showing her the earrings nestled in cotton.

"They're lovely, Peter," Hope's mother told him.

"You really think she'll like them?" he asked anxiously.

"Well, I don't know your mother's taste, of course, but *I* would certainly be thrilled to get them."

"Thanks," Peter said. Hope's mother had great taste, and he felt better having her approval.

"Well, I really have to run," Mrs. Chang said. She hesitated, and then went on, "Peter, Hope has to work late this evening. She claims she doesn't care, but I think she does. If you have the time, maybe you could stop by and wish her a Merry Christmas."

"Uh, yeah, I think I'll have time." If he and Hope hadn't had a fight, nothing would have kept him away. Of course, if she hadn't taken the job in the first place, she wouldn't be stuck here on Christmas Eve, and the fight would never have happened. But Peter decided it wasn't such a good idea to discuss that with Hope's mother. No sense getting stung twice.

He did feel bad for Hope, though, so he said, "Sure, Mrs. Chang, I'll go over there now."

"Miss Chang." Mrs. Randolph, looking her most imperious, stared down her long nose at the scarf table, which was in its usual state — a mess. "I realize that in a few hours, the store will be closed and we'll all be able to go home and enjoy the holiday. But during those few hours, we have work to do."

"Mrs. Randolph." Hope took a deep breath and forced herself to smile. "I had to take care of some customers. I'll straighten the table now."

With a nod, Mrs. Randolph moved off, leaving behind her a scent of perfume that always made Hope's eyes itch. Hope watched her go, and then automatically began straightening the scarves. What had Peter called her? A drill sergeant, that was it. Hope had to admit it, he was right about that.

At the thought of Peter, Hope's shoulders

137

sagged. She knew no couple could go along forever without having an argument, but she'd never expected that she and Peter would have one so soon, especially not such a serious one. What made her so sad, on a day when she shouldn't have been sad at all, was that she thought he understood her better than anyone in the world. And to find out that he didn't, hurt like crazy.

"Miss Chang, you have a customer waiting!"

Hope snapped out of her thoughts and followed Mrs. Randolph's pointing finger. By the time she reached the cash register, three customers had appeared, and they kept Hope too busy to think about Peter.

The last customer, a middle-aged woman who looked completely frazzled, frowned at the paper bag Hope handed to her. "I'd like this scarf gift-wrapped," she said.

"Certainly," Hope said. "The gift-wrap department is on the third floor, right next to the return department."

The woman sighed. "Look, honey, I've been shopping since nine this morning, and I've got corns on both feet. If I have to go upstairs and stand in line for an hour, I'll never even see Christmas Day. Do me a big favor and wrap it here, why don't you?"

"I would if I could, but I don't have any paper here," Hope explained. "But I can give you this." Reaching under the counter, she pulled out one of the collapsible silver cardboard boxes with the name of the store printed on it. Mrs. Randolph had told her they were running low on boxes and she should only give them out to the customers who asked, but this woman *did* look exhausted. "Will this do?" she asked.

The women considered it, and then finally nodded. "I guess it'll have to."

"Good," Hope said with a smile. "And Merry Christmas."

"Ha."

Shaking her head, Hope rushed back to the messy scarf table, automatically checking the wall clock to see how many more hours she had left. It was three o'clock. Four and a half more, and then she could go home. She just hoped her family held off on the tree-trimming until she got there. They'd been awfully upset about her having to work late today, but they wouldn't start Christmas Eve without her. Would they?

"Hope, hi!" Olivia Evans' voice called out. "The last time I saw you here you were doing exactly the same thing!"

Hope looked up from the scarves and saw Olivia standing hand-in-hand with a tall, grinning, husky boy about twice her size. It was Walt Manners. Behind them were Pres Tilford, Patrick Henley, and Angie Poletti.

"Hi," Hope said, laughing. "I guess it *does* look like I haven't made any progress." Smiling, she greeted the others.

"This place is crazy," Walt remarked, looking around at the people elbowing their way by. "What a way to spend Christmas Eve."

"Well, I get off pretty soon," Hope said, unfolding and refolding the same scarf. "And it's not so bad, anyway."

"I knew you were working," Olivia explained, "and I didn't get a chance to wish you a Merry Christmas yesterday, so I wanted to come by and do it today."

"Thanks, Olivia," Hope said. "That was really nice."

"We were thinking of going for something to eat," Angie said, smiling at Hope. "When do you get off? Maybe you could come with us."

"Oh, well, thank you." Hope fumbled with the scarf and started to refold it. "But I won't have time."

"Too bad," Pres said. "You look like you could use a break."

"Well, hey, as long as we're here, we might as well make ourselves useful." Letting go of Olivia's hand, Walt reached for a pile of scarves. "Is there a trick to this?" he asked Hope, "or can any reasonably intelligent person fold these things?"

"Any reasonably intelligent idiot can fold these things," Pres said, taking another pile. "Come on, you guys, let's have a race."

Laughing and joking, the six of them tackled the scarf table.

It was then that Peter walked by. He'd expected to find Hope worn out from following that creepy woman's orders, and miserable at having to even be here in the first place. Maybe he'd even hoped that was how he'd find her, he admitted to himself. If he caught her in that mood, she might be glad to see him, might even be willing to forgive him for whatever he'd done, or at least be willing to talk about it.

But when he saw her standing between Pres Tilford and Patrick Henley, laughing as if she'd just heard the funniest joke in the world, Peter stopped hoping. Whatever she was, she wasn't miserable, and whatever she needed, it wasn't the sight of him. Not right now, anyway, not when she was obviously having the time of her life.

Maybe some other time, Peter thought. Or maybe never. Clasping the box that held his mother's earrings, he turned and left the store.

"That was fun," Angie said. The six young people had made short work of the scarf table, and now the brightly colored scarves were arranged in neat stacks. "Who won?"

"I did," Walt claimed. "I folded exactly twenty-seven scarves in forty seconds flat."

"Then you lose," Patrick told him. "I folded thirty."

"Let's have a recount," Pres suggested.

"No, please!" Hope laughed and spread her arms protectively over the table. "Let's just call it a tie."

"All right, a tie," Walt grumbled good-naturedly. "I accept, under protest."

"Come on, you guys," Olivia said, "I have to be home by five. If we want to get something to eat, we'd better do it now." She turned to Hope.

"See you Monday morning at practice, Hope. Have a great Christmas."

"Thank you, same to you," Hope called after them as they left. She was still smiling over the scarf-folding contest, but as she saw Walt drape an arm over Olivia's shoulder, she frowned. She knew Walt and Olivia had gone together once, but that was all over, wasn't it? Olivia was crazy about David Duffy, Hope knew that, so she couldn't help being confused. Had something happened between them? She hoped not. She thought David and Olivia were perfect for each other.

"Miss Chang!" Mrs. Randolph's near-baritone voice rang out. "Let's not neglect the customers!"

Pasting a smile on her face, Hope nodded to her boss and dashed over to the cash register. Again, she checked the wall clock near the escalators. Three-thirty. Four hours to go. Four more hours of Mrs. Randolph, rude customers, and tinny-sounding Christmas carols.

Like most stores, Langston's piped in holiday music continuously, and the crude, scratchy, warbling sound was beginning to get on Hope's nerves. As she tried not to listen to "Jingle Bells," she found herself thinking of the clear, pure, soothing sounds of her violin.

CHAPTER

If Hope was slightly confused about Olivia
and Walt being together again, then Olivia was
completely baffled. At first it had seemed completely natural, just like old times. Laughing at
his jokes, holding his hand, listening to his
stories — Olivia had fallen into it as easily as if
she'd stepped into a pair of soft, well-worn jeans.

The best thing about it was that there was no
pressure. Walt couldn't have cared less about
Rob Ladd or why he was on the squad. He'd
asked her exactly two questions about it, barely
listening to her answers before he was off on some
other subject. It was such a relief, not having to
lie or make excuses, that ever since Walt had
arrived, Olivia spent every minute she could with
him.

Now, though, as she and Walt, Patrick, Angie,

and Pres left Langston's and searched the mall for someplace not too crowded to eat, Olivia found herself wondering about David. What was he doing? What was he feeling? Where was he right this minute, and did he still have that hurt look in his eyes?

"Hey, this place looks good," Walt said, squeezing her hand and pointing to a sandwich place. "I could go for a ham and swiss, how about you?"

"I just want something to drink," Olivia said. "This'll be fine."

"Well, I'm starving," Angie declared, collapsing into a chair. "I want a hot dog. Two hot dogs, and fries."

"Who's going to stand in line?" Pres asked. The place didn't have waiters.

"You and Patrick and Walt," Olivia informed him with a grin. "You're still standing, so you're elected to get the food. I'll have a Seven-Up with lots of ice."

As soon as the boys had joined the line, Olivia turned to Angie. "I have to talk to you," she said. "Something's driving me crazy, and I don't know what to do about it."

Angie laughed. "If it's driving you crazy, it must be a boy."

"It is," Olivia admitted. "David Duffy."

"I knew it," Angie said. "I had a feeling there was more between you two than you let on the other night."

"There is," Olivia told her. Or there *was*, she thought miserably.

"Then why are you spending so much time with Walt? I don't want to pry," Angie said, "but I couldn't help wondering."

Olivia shrugged her shoulders helplessly. "It's kind of complicated. Part of it has to do with the squad."

Angie frowned. "What is it, does David mind all the time it takes or something?"

"No, nothing like that." Olivia chewed her lip for a second and then went on. "Angie, I can't go into it, but there's trouble on the squad."

"What kind of trouble?" Angie asked, her eyes wide. "Does it have to do with Rob Ladd? I couldn't help noticing that you clam up every time somebody mentions him. I asked Pres about it, but he says nobody's talking."

"We can't talk. We promised," Olivia said. "Trust me, Angie, I'd tell you if I could, but I can't!"

"All right." Angie nodded. "If you promised, I won't bug you, even though I'm still totally confused. But what does this have to do with David?"

"He won't *stop* bugging me," Olivia told her.

"Oh, right," Angie said. "He's a reporter."

Olivia nodded and sighed. "I wish he weren't. If he just didn't ask so many questions, then everything would be fine."

"No, it wouldn't," Angie said thoughtfully. "If he didn't ask so many questions, he wouldn't be David Duffy. And if he weren't David Duffy, you wouldn't love him."

Before Olivia could come up with an answer

to that, the boys returned, their hands full of food and their mouths full of jokes. Olivia joined in the chatter and laughter, losing her worries in the company of her old friends.

If things could just stay this way, she thought as they left the mall and piled into the moving van, then everything would be fine.

Patrick, who was driving the van, suddenly swerved sharply, and Olivia was thrown against Walt, who put his arm around her and pulled her closer.

"Hey, thanks, Patrick," Walt called out jokingly. "I'm much more comfortable now."

Everyone laughed, including Olivia. It was easy, so easy. All she had to do was lean back against Walt, who didn't care a rap about Rob Ladd, and forget about David, who cared too much.

Jessica, standing in the middle of a Christmas tree lot with her mother and Daniel, saw Patrick's van as it rounded the corner and drove out of sight. On top of it, tied with rope at either end, was a beautiful, full, long-needled tree, the kind you usually saw in magazines, gracing a living room filled with expensive furniture and a blazing fireplace.

"Jessica? What do you think?"

Jessica pulled her eyes away from the street and turned back to the business at hand. Her mother was holding a spindly spruce out for inspection. The tree was pathetic. Tall and skinny, its branches were spaced about a foot apart, until the top where there weren't any.

Her mother looked hopeful, and Jessica was trying to find a single good thing to say about the tree, when Daniel spoke up. "Shake it, Abby."

Abby Bennett shook it. A shower of needles rained down, sliding off her coat and piling up on the toes of her boots.

"Too dry," Daniel pronounced. "Put it in a warm house and we might have a case of spontaneous combustion." Laughing, he took it from Abby and leaned it against the fence. He stopped laughing when he looked at the price tag. "Fourteen dollars? They've got to be kidding!"

The tree-lot man, who had been warming himself over a fire in a trash barrel, glanced their way. "Tell you what. I'll give it to you for ten if you'll take it off my hands."

Daniel shook his head. "Thanks," he called, "but I think we can do better."

Jessica wasn't so sure. After all, it was four o'clock on Christmas Eve. All the other tree lots in Tarenton had closed up shop; this was the only one still open, and it had all of fifteen trees left.

"Jessica, how about this one?" her stepfather asked.

"But Daniel, it's missing branches on one whole side," her mother protested.

"So? Half of it's great. It's going in a corner, anyway — the ugly side'll never show."

Jessica stared at the tree, feeling her step-father's impatient eyes on her. "I'd like to look around a little more," she said finally.

Daniel sighed and leaned the tree against the fence. Abby fidgeted and looked at her feet. The tree man shook his head and went back to warming his hands over the flaming trash barrel.

Jessica, feeling very self-conscious, strolled around the tree-lot, carefully inspecting each tree. Why are you taking so much time with this? she asked herself. What difference does it make? On January second, you'll be taking the tree down anyway, so why bother trying to find a good one?

Still, Jessica couldn't stop searching, and as she went from tree to tree, trying to ignore their glaring flaws, she finally realized what she was doing. She was trying to find a tree like the one she'd just seen on top of Patrick's van — a fresh, tall, beautifully symmetrical tree.

Don't be ridiculous, she told herself. You don't find a tree like that in the last lot in Tarenton on the day before Christmas. You have to go to the hills for one of those and chop it down yourself. Just like Patrick did. Just like he invited you to do.

Her boots squeaking on the hard-packed snow, Jessica moved down the line of trees. Her mother and Daniel, she noticed, had joined the tree-lot man at the trash barrel, trying to keep warm. The three of them stood there, hands over the flames, not saying a word to each other. Every few seconds, Daniel would shoot a glance at Jessica, and she could tell by the look in his eyes that he was getting fed up with this entire business.

This is supposed to be fun, Jessica wanted to tell him. Buying a tree should be a fun family outing. Why can't you just relax and enjoy yourself instead of glaring at me and griping at my mother?

Of course, Daniel had inherited a family when he had married Abby, so he wasn't really used to family outings. And there'd been plenty of times when he'd ruined things by not understanding that being part of a family meant that you had to compromise a lot.

But this time, Jessica had to admit that it wasn't Daniel's fault she wasn't having fun. It was hers. Ever since the fight with Patrick, she'd been so moody that everyone tiptoed around her, afraid to set off an explosion. You've been a royal pain in the neck, she told herself. So don't go blaming Daniel because you can't find the perfect tree. And don't blame him because you had a fight with Patrick, either. For once, Daniel doesn't have anything to do with your misery.

The worst part about the fight was that she hadn't expected to feel so bad about it. After all, she'd been honest with Patrick, she hadn't led him on. She'd just told him she didn't want to get involved. *He* was the one who couldn't handle it. So why did she feel like she'd lost something?

"Jessica!" Daniel called. "Find one yet?"

"No," she called back. It was obvious she wasn't going to find one, either. Not today.

"Well, hurry up, will you? Your mother's getting frostbitten out here!"

Forget the tree, Jessica ordered herself. And forget Patrick Henley. You were smart to cut things off with him before they got out of hand. You don't need a perfect tree to have a happy Christmas, and you don't need Patrick to have a happy life.

"No luck," she reported, joining her mother and Daniel at the barrel.

"I figured as much," Daniel said. "I told you we should have bought one a week ago."

"I know," Jessica admitted. "It's my fault. Sorry."

"Well, it doesn't matter, does it?" her mother said anxiously. She held up the tree that had branches missing on one side. "We can make do with this one, can't we?"

"Sure, Mom," Jessica agreed, wondering how long she'd have to make do with missing Patrick. Not long, she hoped. This awful, lost feeling couldn't last very long. "Let's go home and put it up."

All over Tarenton, people were hurrying home, eager to get out of the bitter cold and into the warmth of their houses. Tree lights blinked on and off in picture windows, last-minute gifts were wrapped, even a few hardy carolers made the rounds in some neighborhoods.

At Tara's house, which had a tree and a blazing fireplace almost exactly like the one Jessica had seen in magazines, everything seemed cozy and quiet. For once, Tara's father didn't have a raquetball game lined up, and her mother wasn't entertaining bridge guests, so all three of them were together in the living room.

Tara, stretched out in front of the fireplace, eyed the enormous pile of boxes under the tree, and hoped that some of the ones for her had clothes in them. She'd just finished mentally going over her wardrobe, and nothing seemed quite right for an afternoon buffet at a senator's house.

It was going to be a very interesting party, she thought with a smile. Especially with Sean there. After the other night at Freddy's, she'd realized just how much alike Sean Dubrow and Rob Ladd were. Of course, Rob was a little smoother, a little more subtle about it, but he hadn't fooled Tara for a minute — he was just as cocksure and full of himself as Sean. No wonder the two of them couldn't get along. It was like mixing fire with fire — you just got more fire.

Well, Tara liked both boys, and Tara liked fire. She turned onto her side, her back to the hearth. Yes, it was going to be very interesting, seeing which one of them came out of this unscathed.

At that moment, driving with his father to his grandparents' house a hundred miles from Tarenton, Sean Dubrow was feeling very *un*sure of himself, and it wasn't a feeling he liked at all.

He kept telling himself to forget about Rob and Tara, but somehow he couldn't shake the feeling that he was at a disadvantage.

Sean glanced over at his father, who was driving, and was tempted to talk to him about the problem. But then he changed his mind. Not that Mark Dubrow didn't care — Sean knew he did — but his father liked to keep things light. Heavy discussions were just not his style.

Sean wished he were driving. Ever since he'd gotten his license, he liked to be the one behind the wheel. At least then he felt like he was in control. Now he felt like someone else was calling the shots, and as the car sped along the dark highway, Sean knew it wasn't just his father he was thinking about — it was Robinson Ladd.

Hope reached home at seven forty-five, her cheeks red with cold and her mind still spinning from the dizzy, chaotic last few hours at Langston's.

But her family had kept the pizza warm, and no one made a single remark about her job, or the fact that she'd made them wait. So even though they started late, their Christmas Eve routine of decorating the tree together went off exactly the way it had ever since Hope could remember. There was one difference, of course — Peter. What was going to happen between her and Peter?

* * *

In his apartment, Peter Rayman was thinking the same thing about Hope. He tried not to, especially since he didn't want his mother to catch on that something was wrong. Not only would it make her worry, it would make her worry out loud, and Peter definitely couldn't handle any questions about Hope at the moment. So he put on what he thought was a great cover-up, but inside he couldn't stop wondering what was going to happen.

Seeing his mother's eyes light up as she opened the earrings, and hearing her sigh of relief when she tested the footbath, helped some. But not enough. Not nearly enough.

In the Evans house, Olivia was in the kitchen, helping her mother make cranberry sauce. Olivia hated cranberry sauce, especially the homemade kind, with little pieces of berry in it. But she loved the smell, and besides, washing the berries and boiling them kept her hands busy, so she wasn't gnawing at her fingernails.

Unfortunately, making cranberry sauce didn't keep her mind all that busy, and Olivia couldn't stop thinking about two things: the Varsity Squad and David Duffy.

Had it really only been ten days since Mrs. Engborg announced that Rob Ladd was going to be on the squad? Things had changed so much that it seemed more like ten weeks. The squad was going downhill fast, Olivia knew it. Maybe she'd been wrong, maybe she shouldn't have given in so easily and insisted that they try to help Rob look good. It just wasn't possible. What was happening was that he was making *them* look bad, and she didn't even want to think about the reaction they were going to get at their first game of the new year, when they did one of their "new" routines. The crowd would either laugh or boo, she didn't know which. But there was no way they were going to cheer.

Shaking her head, Olivia dumped a pile of berries into the colander. Running her fingers through them for bruised or mashed ones, she wondered if David had opened his present yet. There were some things she didn't know about David Duffy, she realized, and one of them was whether his family opened their gifts on Christmas Eve or Christmas morning. One thing she did know, though, was that he was an extremely important part of her life, just like the squad, and if she didn't do something about their relationship, it was going to go downhill, too.

Olivia turned the water on, washed the berries, and poured them into a saucepan. Now she could measure some sugar, not a difficult task, but at least it required a minute amount of brainpower — enough to take her mind off things for maybe ten seconds.

Reaching for the measuring cup, Olivia shook her head again, trying to clear it of all unwanted thoughts. After Christmas, she told herself. Maybe after Christmas, everything will be all right.

CHAPTER

14

On the Monday after Christmas, at nine-thirty in the morning, Ardith Engborg watched the cheerleaders file into the gym for practice. *File* was the wrong word, she realized. Straggle was more like it. Gone were Jessica's almost dancelike grace; Olivia's brisk stride; Peter's loose, peppy walk. Even Sean's strut wasn't up to its usual level. And as for Hope, she looked like her last ship had just sunk.

Only Tara and Rob had any energy, but it wasn't the right kind. As the two of them came into the gym together, Tara's bell-like laugh ringing out clearly, Mrs. Engborg couldn't miss the admiring way she looked at Rob.

She was glad that Tara, at least, seemed to accept Rob, but a romance was not exactly the right kind of acceptance. A romance would just complicate things, and complications were not what this group needed, not if it was going to be in decent shape for the first game of the new year.

That was what was worrying Ardith Engborg most: Would the squad be ready for the new year? And she knew it was bothering the rest of the group, too, along with whatever personal problems had cropped up during the vacation.

Her eyes dropped down to the tablet of paper she held on her lap. Covered with arrows and circles and x's, it was the diagram of a new cheer. A new, *easy* cheer, she thought, glancing at Rob Ladd. It wasn't a bad cheer, she knew that. It would have been fine for a beginning group of cheerleaders. But except for Rob, these people were no longer beginners, and they could do this cheer easily.

Six of these cheerleaders were going to hate it, she told herself, and you can't blame them. Especially since *you* hate it yourself. For a moment, Ardith Engborg was tempted to let herself feel all the anger that had been bottled up inside her, ever since Judson Abbott had threatened to get rid of the squad entirely if she didn't put Rob on it. If she let that anger surface, she would have ripped up the new cheer and sent Rob packing.

But she knew she couldn't do it. It would feel terrific for about an hour, but then what? No one needed to tell her the answer to that: No Rob, no squad. And Ardith Engborg had worked too hard — these cheerleaders had worked too hard — to give it up now. With a determined glint in her eye, she took up her pencil and began making some adjustments on the new cheer.

Except for Tara and Rob, the cheerleaders went through their warm-up exercises almost silently. Hope politely thanked Peter for the lovely bracelet, and Peter, wishing she'd at least worn it today, thanked her for the record she'd given him. Then the two of them went to opposite corners of the gym.

Jessica and Olivia, both lost in their own thoughts, bent and stretched their muscles side by side, each hardly noticing that the other was there. Christmas with Daniel hadn't gone as badly as Jessica had expected. In fact, Daniel had been downright jolly, and even though one part of Jessica kept saying that this was what she wanted — a happy family, good friends, and *no* romantic commitments — another part kept saying that something was missing.

Olivia hadn't seen David Duffy for three days. He'd called once, when she was out with Walt, to wish her a Merry Christmas. But when she'd called him back, there was no answer. She'd tried again to thank him for his gift, an antique music box. Still no answer. Either he was visiting relatives, or he was tracking down leads to his "hot" story. Olivia hoped he was visiting relatives.

Sean was once again concentrating hard on ignoring Robinson Ladd. It still seemed the best way to go, but it was beginning to make him very uptight. Stretching his legs with a vengeance, Sean wished the coach would have them do one of their toughest cheers. At least that way he could work off some of this frustration.

"Okay, everybody," Mrs. Engborg called, looking up from her notepad. "I took some time over the weekend, and worked up a new cheer. Doing a new routine from scratch should help all of you feel more like a team."

Fat chance, thought Sean.

"There's no need for me to give you copies of my diagram, because it's not that complicated," the coach went on. "I think it'll be easier if I just talk you through it."

And don't forget to hold Rob's hand, Sean thought.

"I want two lines," Mrs. Engborg directed, "girls in front, boys behind, but in between the girls, so you can be seen."

The cheerleaders took their places, and Sean found himself standing next to Rob Ladd, who had taken the middle position. Sean could have made a point of moving over to the other side of Peter, but that would have looked juvenile, and besides, Peter couldn't stand the guy, either.

"All right," Mrs. Engborg said, "the cheer's in two parts. During the first part, you'll stamp your feet and clap your hands; then in the second part, you'll do some moves with the pompons. First, the words:

"Let's move!
Let's go!
Let's really show,
Who's best,
Who's tops,
Who's number one —
Tarenton!"

It took all of three minutes to memorize, even for Rob. Then came the movements: "move," clap-clap; "go," stamp-stamp; "show," clap *and* stamp.

On the words *best*, *tops*, and *one*, they were to swing their pompons in wide arcs, and finally, on the word *Tarenton*, they got to do a straddle jump.

Mrs. Engborg had been right. It was a simple cheer, but not a bad one. Performed with energy and commitment, it could have looked very good. But if there was any commitment on the squad at the moment, it didn't show, and there was precious little energy.

Pressing her lips into a thin line, she watched the cheerleaders drag themselves through the routine for a minute before she stopped them. "I've seen more bounce in a dead tennis ball," she said. "What's wrong with you people? Counting today, we have exactly eight more practices left before the game with Garrison. Keep working like this, and not even eighty practices will get you ready."

No one said a word. The coach was obviously angry, and not even Rob Ladd was tempted to come out with a smooth remark. The only thing they could think of to do was stare at their feet.

Mrs. Engborg watched them watching their feet, and then she started to go on. "This is an easy cheer — "

"That's the problem," Sean broke in. He hadn't meant to say it, but it was too late now. The coach raised an eyebrow and gave him a very cold look.

"Please, Sean, explain what you mean by that."

"I mean it's *too* easy," Sean said bluntly. "It's no fun. Couldn't we add a couple more moves to it? Maybe Peter and I could do back flips instead of straddle jumps."

"Wait a minute," Jessica said. "That leaves Olivia and me out in the cold. If you guys get to do back flips, then we should, too."

"Fine with me," Sean said, with a trace of his old grin. "Let's try it."

"Let's not." Mrs. Engborg stared at them sternly. She understood their frustration. She even shared it. But if she let them take over, then Rob Ladd would be the one left out in the cold, and she couldn't let that happen. "Back in line, please," she instructed. "And do the cheer as written."

Before the cheerleaders could respond, the gym door opened and Judson Abbott walked in. He flashed a warm smile toward the group of young people, then headed straight for the coach and spoke quietly and intensely for a moment.

Ardith Engborg listened, nodded, and turned to the squad. "I have to step out for a few minutes," she said. "Olivia, you've got the cheer down, don't you?"

Olivia nodded. Who wouldn't? she thought.

"Fine, then take over while I'm gone, please. And when I come back, I hope I see some improvement."

After Abbott and the coach had gone, Sean whistled softly. "Well, well," he remarked, "I wonder what the young, up-and-coming politician wants this time."

"Sean," Olivia said with a warning glance. "Don't start."

"Don't start what?" Sean asked. "I'm just curious, that's all. Seems to me that Judson Abbott is spending a lot of valuable time here in the halls of Tarenton High. Doesn't anybody else want to know why?"

Olivia was as curious as Sean was, but seeing the way he kept glancing at Rob Ladd, she didn't think it would be such a great idea to have a group discussion about Judson Abbott.

Putting her hands on her hips, she faced Sean. "You heard what the coach said," she told him. "Let's get back to work."

Tiny as she was, there weren't many people who would argue with Olivia Evans when she got that glint in her eye, and Sean wasn't one of them. Somehow, the sight of Judson Abbott was like a dose of megavitamins — it had snapped Sean out of his blue mood and filled him with quick energy. But it wasn't enough to make him tangle with Olivia.

Throwing up his hands, he said, "Okay, Captain. Let's see if we can do the impossible."

"What do you mean, the impossible?" Tara asked.

"Pump life into a dead cheer," Sean replied, and got in position.

The others followed, and with Olivia shouting out the words, they started rehearsing.

> "Let's move! (clap, clap)
> Let's go!" (stamp, stamp)

They got through the first part without a hitch. They even put a little zip into it, Olivia noticed. It wasn't much, but it was better than nothing.

> "Who's best, (swing the pompons)
> Who's tops. . . ."

That's when it happened. No one knew exactly what went wrong, but somehow, Rob's and Sean's pompons collided, the red and white plastic strands tangling like windblown hair.

It would have been funny — the two boys standing there, tugging at their pompons, trying to pull them apart. But neither boy was looking at what he was doing; instead they were looking each other in the eye, and the expressions on their faces were not laughable. If the pompons had been swords, someone would have been cut.

Rob spoke first. "I'm almost certain we were supposed to swing to the right on 'tops,'" he said.

"True," Sean agreed calmly. "There's just one problem."

"Oh?"

Sean nodded, not taking his eyes off Rob. "Yeah, it's a common problem: learning your left from your right. Most people master it by the time they're in kindergarten, but a few others take longer."

"Okay," Oliva said, trying to sound as much like Ardith Engborg as she could, "let's just do it again."

"I agree," Hope put in. "It doesn't matter what went wrong. Let's just get it right."

"Wait a minute." Rob held out his hand, but kept his eyes on Sean. "Let me tell you something, Dubrow."

"Be my guest."

Cocking a sandy eyebrow, Rob gave Sean one of his laziest smiles. "I just wanted to say that if you're one of those people who's had trouble mastering left from right, I'll be glad to set you straight."

"Come on, you guys," Peter said. "This is getting boring."

Neither Sean nor Rob heard him. They'd started tugging at the pompons again, trying to separate them. They were pulling with such force that when they finally succeeded, both of them fell backward onto the floor.

Scrambling up immediately, they squared off like boxers in a ring.

"I don't think you understand, Ladd," Sean said softly. "You're the one who needs the tutoring, not me."

"Not 'I,'" Rob corrected.

"Okay, okay!" Olivia said. "Forget it, both of you. This is ridiculous."

"I agree," Rob said with a nod. "It *is* ridiculous." Slowly, he moved closer to Sean until they were just inches apart. "What do you say Dubrow? Are you ready to call a truce?"

Sean might have laughed the whole thing off if it hadn't been for the smirk on Rob Ladd's face. That smirk got to him, and he couldn't help himself. Goaded, he placed his fingertips on Rob's chest and gave a slight plush. "Truce?" he asked. Another push. "If there's going to be a truce, then I'll have to see a flag." Another light push. "Where's the white flag, Ladd?"

Rob didn't touch Sean, but his eyes were hard and cold, exactly the way Tara had seen them at Freddy's Diner. "But Dubrow," he said, "I thought *you* had them all."

Sean was just about ready to let go and give Rob a real shove, when Mrs. Engborg's voice rang out, as cold and hard as Rob's eyes: "What's the meaning of this?"

Everyone else had been so sure a fight was about to erupt, that they couldn't drag their attention away from the two opponents in time to answer the coach. But Rob, for once, was quick on his feet. "Just a disagreement, Mrs. Engborg." His voice was as smooth as silk. "A very small disagreement."

"It didn't look small to me," the coach commented. Then, looking only at Sean, she said, "I expected more of you, Sean. I'm very disappointed."

Sean felt the way he had when he was eight years old and his playground buddy had hopped off the seesaw while Sean was still up in the air. His breath went out of him in one big whoosh, leaving him lightheaded and sick to his stomach. Was the coach actually taking Ladd's side in this?

But Sean didn't get a chance to answer or defend himself. Dismissing him with a glance, Mrs. Engborg turned to the captain of the squad. "Olivia, I want to see you in my office." To the rest of them she said, "Practice is over. Be prepared to work overtime tomorrow."

Olivia followed the coach out of the gym and down the eerily empty hall, her sneakers squeaking on the polished tiled floor. It was like going from the frying pan into the fire, she thought, and she wasn't sure which was worse — watching a fight between Sean and Rob, or getting chewed out by Mrs. Engborg. And she was definitely going to get chewed out, she knew that as surely as she knew her left from her right.

Mrs. Engborg didn't waste any time. "Olivia," she said, as she closed the door to her small office,

"I'm disappointed in you, too. You're the captain of the squad. It's up to you to keep things running smoothly when I'm not there. Instead, I come back and find Sean and Rob circling each other like two wrestlers trying to go for a hammerlock."

"I'm sorry," Olivia said. It was all she could think of. "It happened fast and it was . . . a very intense situation. I won't let it happen again."

"I hope not," the coach replied. "But that's not why I called you out," she went on. "There's something else I want to discuss with you, something Judson Abbott brought to my attention."

For a second, Olivia felt a surge of hope. Maybe Abbott had relented. Maybe, somehow, Rob was going to be off the squad.

But when Mrs. Engborg spoke, Olivia's stomach twisted for the first time in days, because it wasn't Rob's name that she mentioned. With a sharp look, the coach said, "I'd like to speak to you about David Duffy."

CHAPTER

15

Olivia's mouth went dry. There was a strange, far-away roaring in her ears, and for a minute, she couldn't speak. Had something terrible happened to David?

Finally, she found her voice. "What is it, Mrs. Engborg?" she asked, visions of a car wreck flashing through her mind. "What's wrong?"

The coach picked up a newspaper from her desk and held up the sports page for Olivia to see.

The headline wasn't hard to miss: MYSTERY SURROUNDS EXPANSION OF TARENTON HIGH VARSITY SQUAD. Underneath that, in smaller type, were the lines, *When It Comes To Cheerleaders, More Is Less.*

The article carried David Duffy's byline, and for a moment, Olivia felt only relief that he was all right. Then she saw Mrs. Engborg watching her, and she quickly scanned the article.

David didn't mince words. Why had the best cheerleading squad in the tri-state region suddenly decided to add a new member? Neither the cheerleaders nor their coach would give a satisfactory answer. And given the facts that the new member was Robinson Ladd, son of a senator, and that Judson Abbott, a well-known local politician, was often seen watching the squad practice, the writer of the article was curious about whether some kind of connection could be made.

There was also the strange fact that Robinson Ladd was not on the same level as the rest of the cheerleaders. "A lame horse trying to run with the thoroughbreds," was how the article put it.

David wove the two themes — why Rob was on the squad, and how the squad was slipping — together throughout the article, ending with a twist on an old saying: "It wasn't broken, so who fixed it? And why?"

If Olivia hadn't been so involved, she would have found the story fascinating. The problem was, however, that they were on vacation, so not that many people had known or cared about Rob Ladd. But now, thanks to David, everyone would know, and everyone would be asking questions.

She looked at Mrs. Engborg. Why had the coach singled her out on this? she wondered. Because she was David's girlfriend, of course. But what did the coach expect her to do? She could hardly tell David to stop investigating the story. First of all, he wouldn't do it. And second, wasn't there some kind of law against interfering with the press?

As if she could read Olivia's mind, Ardith Engborg smiled and shook her head. "Don't worry, Olivia, I wouldn't even think of suggesting that you try to persuade David to stop. But it's a tricky situation."

Olivia nodded.

"I'm all for freedom of the press," the coach went on, "but I can't help wishing this reporter wasn't quite so observant."

"I know what you mean," Olivia said.

"He's persistent, too," Mrs. Engborg remarked, her lips twitching in amusement. "A little too persistent for Judson Abbott's taste. It seems that David Duffy has been pestering Abbott with some very pointed questions. In fact, he was waiting outside Abbott's office this morning, which is why Mr. Abbott showed up at practice earlier. He told me, in so many words, to put a lid on David Duffy."

Olivia laughed. She couldn't help it. No one put a lid on David Duffy.

"It *is* funny," the coach agreed. "Or it would be if. . . ." Her words trailed off, and for a moment she just stared at the desktop.

For the first time since this mess began, Olivia realized the pressure that Mrs. Engborg was under. This isn't fair, she thought, feeling furious and helpless at the same time.

"What do you . . . I mean, is there anything

that you want me to do?" she asked, still wondering why Mrs. Engborg had called her into the office.

Ardith Engborg shook her head again. "I thought it was only fair to tell you that I'm going to keep our practices closed from now on. No more Judson Abbott. No more David Duffy." She stood up quickly, some of her usual briskness returning. "That much, I can do. I just didn't want you to think that I'm opposed to what David's doing, or that I'm out to get him. But I do have the squad to think of. Do you understand?"

Olivia understood. The squad was terribly important to her, too. "Don't worry, Mrs. Engborg," she said. "I think it's a good idea to have closed practices. Maybe we'll get more work done."

"I hope so," the coach told her. "We need it."

Olivia couldn't argue with that, and since there didn't seem to be anything more to say, she left the office and went back to the locker room to change.

Hope had already left, but Tara and Jessica had just finished their showers. Both girls looked up expectantly when Olivia came in.

"Well?" Tara asked, her blue eyes wide. "What happened?"

"Nothing much," Olivia said.

"What do you mean, nothing much?" Tara looked disappointed. "You mean she didn't ask you about the fight?"

The fight. Olivia had almost forgotten about Sean and Rob. "Oh. No, not really."

"Well, what did she want?" Tara insisted.

Obviously, neither Tara nor Jessica had seen David's article yet. Olivia was just as glad. She wasn't in the mood to discuss it. But there was something she did want to discuss. "The coach told me to be a better captain," she said.

"You're a great captain," Tara said indignantly.

Jessica frowned and leaned against a bank of lockers. "What did she mean by that, Olivia?"

"She meant that somebody has to be the leader, and since I'm captain, I'm the one." Looking pointedly at Jessica, Olivia went on. "I know nobody likes Rob being on the squad, but it's time we got used to it. It's time we started working. All of us."

Jessica pushed herself away from the lockers, opened hers, and took out her sneakers. "I've been working," she said, tossing the shoes down.

"I mean working together," Olivia told her. "We can't keep letting Rob make mistakes. If we do, the whole squad is going to be laughed out of the gym."

Jessica was tying her shoes and didn't look up. "Does that mean you're going to work with him, Olivia?"

"Not just me," Olivia said. "All of us. We're all going to work with him, and we're going to make him look as good as we can." She took a deep breath. "I want us to get here half an hour early tomorrow," she announced, "so we can get something done before the coach comes."

"But Mrs. Engborg already told us we had to work extra tomorrow," Tara protested. "Why should we come in early?"

"Because I say so."

"Does Mrs. Engborg know about this?" Jessica asked.

"No," Olivia said, "but she told me to be a better captain, Jessica, and that's what I'm going to do."

For a minute, Olivia was afraid that Jessica might refuse to come. After all, Olivia didn't really have any power, and she knew that Jessica was completely against helping Rob Ladd.

But Jessica surprised her by not arguing. She finished tying her shoes, stood up, and pulled on her jacket. "All right," she said with a nod. "See you tomorrow morning at nine." Without another word, she left the locker room.

"Well, that's a relief," Tara remarked after she'd gone. "But I bet you won't be able to talk Sean into coming early or helping Rob." Laughing, she pulled on a bright yellow sweater and a pair of brown corduroy pants. "Could you believe that scene this morning? I really thought there was going to be a fight, didn't you?"

"You sound disappointed that there wasn't," Olivia said.

Surprised, Tara stopped and dropped one of her buttery soft leather boots. "What does that mean?"

"Come on, Tara." Olivia couldn't help smiling. "It's so obvious that you get a big kick out of seeing Rob and Sean go at each other."

"That's not true," Tara claimed. "Do you really think I wanted them to beat each other up?"

"Well, maybe not that," Olivia admitted. "But you like Rob, and you like Sean, and since they hate each other's guts, it makes it interesting for you, doesn't it? It's sort of like a game with you."

Olivia was very close to the truth, but Tara wasn't about to admit it. Pulling on her boots, she stood up and grabbed her yellow canvas bag. "I don't think it's any of your business."

"You'd be right, except for one thing," Olivia said. "The squad. You're playing games with Sean and Rob, Sean's getting madder by the minute, and that hurts the squad."

"Oh, I forgot," Tara said sarcastically. "This is all for the squad. Anything for the squad, right?"

"Right," Olivia said instantly. "I didn't think I'd have to tell you that."

When Tara had gone, Olivia tiredly peeled off her sweat clothes, and stepped into the shower. The warm spray pounded some of the soreness out of her muscles, but it didn't do a thing for the tension in her mind.

Some captain you are, she told herself. You just got two members of the squad mad at you, ordering them around like they were servants or something, and now you expect them to show up tomorrow with smiles on their faces. Well, they'll show up, all right, but they won't be smiling. And that's not going to help the squad one bit.

Olivia turned around in the shower stall, letting the water roll off her back. Tara had been right about one thing: Just how was she going to convince Sean to cooperate with Rob Ladd? She might as well ask him to cooperate with a rattlesnake. She'd just have to keep her fingers crossed that Sean cared enough about the squad to at least try.

And what about David? Could she talk him into backing off the story without telling him why? Should she even try?

Better not, she decided, turning the shower off and wrapping a fluffy blue towel around herself. All you'll do is make him more determined than he already is. Better just leave him alone and hope he never finds the solution to his "mystery."

At least Walt's still here, Olivia thought. And tonight, you can let him tell you so many crazy jokes that you'll forget about everything. Until tomorrow.

Jessica was halfway to the bus stop when she heard a car honking behind her. She remembered the time Patrick had honked at her after practice, not too long ago. That's when they'd had their fight.

Jessica kept on walking. It couldn't be Patrick this time, she thought. If he was still as angry as he had been, then he'd hardly offer her a ride home.

Thinking of Patrick made Jessica remember the present he'd given her. Before the fight, of course. It was a necklace, the links so tiny and delicate that they looked like they'd been cut out of gold paper. It was a beautiful piece of jewelry, and Jessica loved it. The problem was, what to do about it? Should she keep it, or give it back?

"Jessica!" someone called. "Hey, Jessica!"

Turning, Jessica saw a red Porsche creeping along close to the curb, with Pres Tilford at the wheel, waving at her. "Want a lift?" he called.

"Sure!" she called back, and trotted over to the car. Sinking into the soft leather seat, she smiled at him. "Thanks. This is a great way to travel."

"My feeling exactly," Pres said with a grin, and putting the car into gear, he peeled away from the curb. "Speaking of feelings," he went on, "how are you these days?"

"Fine," Jessica said quickly. "We had a nice Christmas, how about you?"

"Not bad," Pres told her. "But that isn't what I meant."

"Oh?"

He shook his head. "Jessica, you can tell me this is none of my business and I wouldn't blame you, but I was wondering what's going on with you and Patrick."

Jessica hesitated. She really didn't want to discuss the situation, but she didn't want to be rude, either. After all, Pres was Patrick's good friend. He cared about him.

"Nothing's going on," she said finally. "We ... had a fight."

"Do you mind if I ask what it was about?"

"You mean Patrick didn't tell you?"

"Nope. Well, he told me you had a fight, but he wouldn't go into it. He just said the two of you decided not to see each other so much."

"Oh." Jessica took a deep breath. "That's not quite true. I was the one who decided it, not Patrick."

Pres nodded and then grinned at her again. "Here comes another nosy question: Why?"

"I ... I just don't want to get involved," Jessica said.

"With Patrick?"

"With anybody." Jessica looked out the window at the snowy yards. Then, so softly that Pres could harly hear her, she said, "But if I did want to, it would be with Patrick."

Pres nodded again. "Well, that makes sense. I mean, Patrick's a great guy. What doesn't make sense is why you don't want to get involved."

Jessica turned from the window, her green eyes bright. "Did he ask you to talk to me?"

"Are you kidding?" Pres laughed and shook his head. "If he knew I was doing this, he'd buy my half of the moving business and run me out of town."

Jessica thought she'd be relieved, but instead

she felt disappointed. If Patrick had asked Pres to talk to her, then that would mean he still cared. But he hadn't, so he didn't. But that's what she wanted, wasn't it? So why was she disappointed?

"I just decided to take a chance and talk to you on my own," Pres was saying. "Because, to tell you the truth, Patrick's the most miserable mover-garbage collector in the entire town of Tarenton."

"He is?"

"Sure," Pres said. "He's so low, he's getting things backwards — he's moving garbage and taking people's perfectly good furniture to the dump."

Without thinking, Jessica laughed.

"I hope you're laughing at my joke," Pres told her, "not at Patrick's misery."

"I'm not laughing at either one of them," Jessica said, and laughed again.

"I'm confused."

"So am I, Pres. So am I."

After a still-confused Pres dropped her off, Jessica let herself into the empty house and headed straight for the living room. The tree was still up, its branchless side facing a corner. Underneath it were a few gifts that no one had put away yet: a basket filled with different kinds of jams, a box of scented soaps, a brain-teaser puzzle that no one had been able to solve.

There was also a small white box nestled on the circle of green felt that Jessica's mother used to cover up the tree stand. Jessica picked it up and opened it. Inside was the necklace Patrick had given her.

Lifting the fine gold chain from its bed of cotton, Jessica fingered the necklace and tried to understand what she was feeling.

Pres had said that Patrick was miserable, which meant he still cared about her. That's why Jessica had laughed. Patrick cared and that made her happy, happy enough to laugh out loud, happier than she'd ever felt in her life. This was not the way she was supposed to feel, but she couldn't stop. And she wasn't sure she even wanted to stop.

Still holding the necklace, Jessica went into the hall, stood in front of the oval mirror, and stared at herself. Then, slowly and carefully, she slipped the necklace over her head, letting it settle around her neck.

CHAPTER

"All right, Olivia," Hope said over the phone. "No, it isn't a problem, really. I'll be there at nine. You're welcome. 'Bye."

Hanging up the kitchen phone, Hope tightened the belt on her soft blue bathrobe. Then she went to the refrigerator, took out the milk, and poured some into a glass. Sitting at the table, she took a sip, then tried to figure out what she was going to do. It was ten o'clock at night; surely she could come up with a solution before morning.

Having practice moved up half an hour wasn't a problem at all. Hope was an early-riser, she always had been. There was something about the mornings that made her feel like she could do just about anything. Besides, she knew Olivia was right — the squad had to start working together.

When Hope had tried out for cheerleading, she hadn't been particularly interested in it. It had been her mother's idea. Cheerleading was something her mother had always wanted to do and since she hadn't, she wanted her daughter to do it. Hope had complied, as always, but she'd done it without much enthusiasm.

Now, though, that she'd been a part of the team for so many months, working hard to make it the best, Hope found that she loved it. And if getting to practice half an hour early would keep the squad from falling apart, then she'd be the first to arrive.

No, the problem was what was going to happen *after* practice. Hope had to hurry to get to Langston's as it was, but now that Mrs. Engborg was going to keep them later, to make up for the time they'd lost today, she knew she'd never make it to work on schedule.

Hope took another sip of milk, still not sure how to handle it. If Mrs. Randolph were approachable, she could explain the situation to her. Unfortunately, Mrs. Randolph was about as approachable as a polar bear.

"Hope?" Mrs. Chang came into the kitchen, smiling. "If you're hungry, we have plenty of fruitcake."

Hope laughed. Baking fruitcake for the holidays was one of her mother's passions. Unfortunately, no one in the family except James really liked it, so they wound up giving most of it away. "Thank you, Mother," she said, "but the milk's fine."

"I think I'll join you." Mrs. Chang poured some milk for herself, then sat down at the table and rubbed her eyes. Caroline Chang was a painter and her eyes often bothered her after only a few hours at the easel during the day.

"Did you get much work done today, Mother?" Hope asked.

"Almost nothing," her mother said. "The light's so bad these days. I wish we'd get some sun. It's very frustrating, not being able to do what you want to do."

Hope nodded and drank some more milk. There was only one solution, she decided. She'd have to leave practice twenty minutes early. Of course, that would mean getting to work twenty minutes late, but at least it was an even split.

"I can hear the wheels turning in your head," her mother commented. "What is it?"

"Oh, something that just came up," Hope told her.

"Something with Peter?" Mrs. Chang asked softly.

Hope shook her head. She didn't want to talk about Peter.

But her mother obviously did. "You and Peter had a . . . a falling out, didn't you, Hope?"

"Yes." Hope kept her eyes on her milk glass, wishing her mother wouldn't go on.

"I'm so sorry," Mrs. Chang said.

Hope looked up, surprised. "You are?"

"Of course I am, Hope. Why wouldn't I be?"

"But I thought . . . I mean, you and Father don't really like Peter, do you?" Hope asked. "Because he's not Asian."

Mrs. Chang looked uncomfortable. "It wasn't that we didn't like him, Hope. You're right, though, we did think it would be better for you to see someone of your own kind. But," she went on, "we were wrong. And since then, we've come to realize how much Peter cares about you."

Hope felt a lump in her throat and a prickling feeling in her eyes, but she fought them both. She hated crying. It never helped anything; it just made your eyes red.

"Hope, I know you don't want to discuss your job anymore, so I won't ask you to do it," Mrs. Chang told her daughter. "But it was something Peter said that made your father and me see him in a different light."

Hope waited, wondering what magical words Peter could have spoken to suddenly make her parents forget that he wasn't "one of them."

"He said he wished you'd never taken the job," her mother went on. "And it wasn't because it took you away from him, although I certainly wouldn't blame him for that. It was because he thought you'd be much happier doing what you really love to do."

Smiling again, Mrs. Chang reached out and touched Hope's hand. "Peter knows you, Hope. And he cares for the girl he knows, not the girl you're trying to be."

After her mother left the kitchen, Hope rinsed out the glasses and put them in the dishwasher. She went upstairs, brushed her teeth, and got into bed. It was almost eleven; she knew she should go to sleep. Tomorrow was going to be a tough day.

But she was restless, and even though she tried to clear her mind, she couldn't stop thinking about some of the things her mother had said. Was it really all right just to be herself? To read and play music and just enjoy being alone, instead of trying to change and be more like everyone else? Was that what Peter had been trying to tell her these past few days?

Sitting up, Hope fluffed her pillow, leaned back against the headboard, and stared across the room. Propped against the desk was her violin case. She hadn't touched the violin during the entire vacation, and she suddenly found herself missing the feel and smell of it, the way it became a part of her when she played it, and especially the sounds it made when she pulled the bow across it.

Hope wasn't sure about much at the moment, but one thing she was certain of: It *was* frustrating when you couldn't do what you wanted to do.

The next morning, at eight-thirty, Olivia rounded the corner and walked quickly toward the high school, her breath leaving little cloudy puffs in the cold air. She wanted to be early to prove to everyone that she was serious about working hard, which she was. She also wanted time to figure out exactly what they were going to do for half an hour — she'd been out so late with Walt that she'd fallen into bed without giving it a single thought.

At least everyone had agreed to come at nine, even Sean. She'd sort of tiptoed around the whole thing with him, not mentioning that it was her idea to start practice early. She'd just said that the time had been changed, which was true, and he hadn't argued.

Hitching her cassette recorder a little higher, Olivia headed for the side door that was closer to the gym. Then she stopped in her tracks, not sure whether to laugh or scream.

Outside the door stood a tall boy, wearing jeans and a puffy down jacket. There was nothing unusual about that. What was unusual was what he had on his head — a plaid hat with earflaps tide on top, and long sloping brims in the front and back. A Sherlock Holmes hat. *Her* Sherlock Holmes hat, now being worn by David Douglas Duffy.

Catching sight of Olivia, David grinned. "Hey, Livvy," he called. "I love it! It's perfect! How did you know that I've wanted one of these hats ever since I read *The Hound of the Baskervilles*?"

"I didn't," Oliva answered with a laugh. He really did look funny in it. Funny, but great. "But when I saw it, I just knew it was you."

David laughed, too, and spread his arms wide.

Without thinking, Olivia ran into them and let him pull her close to him. It felt wonderful. *He* felt wonderful.

"Thanks, Olivia," David said, his lips against her hair. "It's the best present I've ever gotten."

Olivia smiled. "Thank you, David, for the music box. I love it." Pulling back, she kissed him lightly. "What are you doing here, anyway?" she asked.

"What do you mean? I'm waiting for squad practice," David told her. "Most of my leads have dried up, and I thought I'd better go back to the source."

"Oh." Frowning, Olivia pulled farther away from the circle of his arms.

"I'm not sure I like the sound of that," David said. "That was definitely not a happy 'oh.'"

"You're right," Olivia admitted. "I guess you don't know."

"Know what?"

"We're having closed practices from now on," Olivia said. "Mrs. Engborg decided we'd get more done that way."

"Ah ha." David tilted the Holmes hat back on his head and folded his arms. "Tell me, Miss Evans, is that the real reason she decided to close the practices? Or did she just want to keep a certain inquiring reporter out?"

"Don't start, David," Olivia said. "For your information, she wanted to keep Judson Abbott out, too."

David's eyes sparkled like sapphires. "Then you admit that 'getting more done' isn't the only reason she's shutting me out."

"I'm not admitting anything," Olivia said hotly. "Stop putting words in my mouth." She took a few steps away from him, and then turned to face him again. "You know, David, if you'd just back off, things might turn out okay."

"What things?" David asked. "The squad? You're not suggesting that I'm the one who's ruining the squad, I hope."

"The squad isn't ruined!" Olivia cried. "Don't say that!"

"Why not? You're doing cheers that were done twenty years ago: 'Lean to the left, lean to the right, stand up, sit down, fight, fight, fight.'" David shook his head. "It rhymes, but that's about all it does. You were the one who turned me on to cheerleading, Olivia. You said it was a sport. And when I saw you guys in action, I knew what you meant. But now?" He shook his head again and adjusted the hat. "Now you look like a bunch of kids hopping up and down. You're not hopping up and down very well, either, and you know it."

"We will," Olivia said. "You'll see. Just give us a chance, David, and stop asking so many questions."

"I'm sorry, but I think the questions are important. I think they need to be answered."

Olivia nodded. She hadn't meant to get into

it with him, and now she wanted out. "Okay," she said. "I know. It's your job." Turning, she reached for the door handle.

"Wait a minute, Livvy."

Olivia turned back and looked into David's blue eyes. There was anger in them, but there was also confusion, and hurt. "There's something we didn't settle," he said. "You said things might be okay if I just backed off. If you didn't mean the squad, what did you mean? Us?"

Olivia just looked into his eyes, not answering.

"Because if that *is* what you meant," David said, "then I don't know what to say. As far as I'm concerned, this story doesn't have a thing to do with you and me. I feel the same way about you that I always have. But you've changed, and I don't know why."

Olivia swallowed hard. She still couldn't think of anything to say.

"I wish you'd tell me," David said. "If I've ruined things between us, don't you think I should know why?" Reaching up, he took off the Holmes hat and looked at it, smiling. "The 'Mystery of the Tarenton High Varsity Squad' is going to be hard enough to solve. Can't you at least give me a few clues to the 'Evans-Duffy mystery'?"

Olivia smiled, too, even though she felt more like crying. "There isn't any 'Evans-Duffy mystery,' David."

"Whew! What a relief!" David exclaimed. "You mean I've just been imagining things?"

"What things?"

"Oh, that you've been avoiding me," he told her. "That you've been seeing Walt Manners instead of me."

"I told you about Walt when he got here," Olivia said uneasily. "I never tried to hide that from you." At least that was one thing she wasn't keeping from David, she thought.

"I know you did," David agreed. "But that's not what I said. I said you've been seeing Walt *instead* of me. And that you've been avoiding me. Isn't that what you've been doing?"

Olivia shook her head, feeling miserable. Not putting it into words made it seem a little less like lying. But it was lying, just the same, and Olivia was sick of it.

David moved close, put his arms around her, and pulled her against him again. His jacket was cold against her cheek, and his breath ruffled her hair. Olivia slipped her arms around his waist, and they stood like that for a minute, not saying anything.

"Can't you tell me what the problem is, Livvy?" David asked finally. "Maybe I can help."

Olivia shook her head again.

"What's that mean — you can't tell or I can't help?"

"Both."

"Then there really *is* a problem, isn't there?" he said. "I mean, if we can't trust each other, then — "

"You don't understand!" Olivia cried, pulling away from him in frustration. "You just don't understand!"

David's eyes flashed. "Then explain it to me!"

"There's nothing to explain!"

"You just said there was!"

"I was wrong," Olivia said. "I mean, I. . . . Oh, forget it, please. Okay? Let's just forget it. I've got to get to practice."

"Right." Nodding, David jammed the new hat back on his head. "Okay, Olivia. We'll forget it. For now. But I'm not going to give up, you know that. On the story, or on you."

Sighing, Olivia watched him walk away, his breath frosting in the air. She wished they could have stood with their arms around each other forever, not saying a word. As long as they didn't talk, she thought wryly, everything was rosy and wonderful.

Suddenly there was a screech, followed by a series of pops, sort of like a very large, very angry bird imitating a firecracker. Olivia dragged her eyes away from David's retreating figure, and looked toward the school parking lot.

A faded green VW bug, decorated with patches of rust, jerked in and screeched to a halt, shuddering as the driver turned it off. The door opened and Rob Ladd got out. Catching sight of Olivia, he raised a hand and waved.

Olivia waved back, glad that she didn't have to talk to him yet. As far as she was concerned,

Rob Ladd was the villain in this piece. Unfortunately, it had been her big idea to call an early practice and help him out. But as she pulled open the door and walked toward the gym, Olivia knew she would be very happy if she never had to lay eyes on him again in her life.

CHAPTER

Accompanied by the loud, throbbing beat of heavy rock music that bounced and echoed off the gymnasium walls, the seven cheerleaders bent and stretched their muscles, warming up for practice.

The music had been Olivia's idea. She'd turned the volume on her tape recorder so high it was impossible for anyone to talk. That had been the point. She figured that if no one could talk, no one could fight. So what if they all went temporarily deaf? It was worth it to keep the peace.

Besides, they hadn't had music during warm-ups in a while, and sometimes it helped loosen up their minds the way the exercises loosened up their bodies. As far as Olivia was concerned, this group needed all the help it could get.

Seated on the floor, her legs apart, Olivia

touched her forehead to her left knee. Straightening, she started to bend to her right knee, but then she decided to take a quick glance at the rest of the squad, sort of a weather-check, to see what the mood was like.

Maybe the music was working, because there didn't seem to be any storms brewing. Not yet, anyway, she thought, looking closely at Sean.

Off in a corner, Sean was doing his warm-ups with so much concentration that he didn't seem to hear the music or see the people around him. He didn't look happy, but at least he didn't look like he was spoiling for a fight.

Olivia stretched forward and sat up again, her eyes on Rob this time. Managing to look handsome even in his ragged gray sweat clothes, Rob seemed to be having a great time. His thin lips were curved in a smile, but it was a genuine smile, not the kind of smile he used when he was egging Sean on. At least, Olivia thought, it *looks* like a genuine smile. She realized that she hadn't even spoken ten words to the guy since he'd joined the team. No one had really, except Sean. And Tara.

Tara's mood was easy to read. Actually it wasn't one mood, it was two. First, she was obviously still slightly miffed about what Olivia had said yesterday. It was obvious because she didn't look *at* Olivia, she looked *through* her. When Tara noticed Rob, though, she was all smiles.

Olivia had meant what she said about Tara playing games with Sean, and she hoped that once Tara got tired of pouting, she'd think about what she was doing. Fooling around with other people's feelings was like playing with matches. Somebody could get burned, and it just might be the person who started the fire.

But Olivia wasn't really that worried about Tara at the moment. Or about Hope. Hope was one of the best things that had happened to the squad. She was a good cheerleader, she always gave her best, and she was loyal.

Hope was looking nervous, Olivia noticed, but it probably didn't have anything to do with cheerleading. It probably had to do with Peter, who was looking miserable. Something must have gone wrong between those two, Olivia thought, wondering what it was and how long it had been going on. You've really gotten out of touch, she told herself.

Sighing, Olivia looked across at Jessica, wondering if the two of them would ever be in touch. It was too bad that they disagreed about the squad; it seemed to be ruining their chances of becoming real friends. At least Jessica had showed up early, like she'd said she would, Olivia thought. Probably called me names all the way over here.

Then Olivia looked more closely at the tall, graceful girl, and realized she was completely wrong about her mood. Like Sean, Jessica was doing her warm-ups as if she were in a world of her own. But instead of a grudging, "well, all right, you're the captain" attitude, she had a strange, almost frightened look on her face, as if she were getting ready to do something dangerous. Olivia couldn't imagine what she was thinking about, and she decided that Jessica Bennett was a real mystery.

The word mystery immediately made her think of David Duffy. Don't even start, she told herself. If you start thinking about David, you'll crawl into a corner and cry. Which is not what the captain of a Varsity Squad does.

Action, she thought. Action will help you shut David out of your mind. Leaping to her feet, Olivia walked quickly over to her tape recorder and pressed the stop button, cutting the music off in midblast.

In the ringing silence that followed, she said, "Let's work on the cheer we were doing yesterday. Everybody remember their positions?"

Everybody did, and they got ready without a word.

"Let's move!
Let's go!
Let's really show. . . ."

The cheerleaders moved, went, and showed with more energy than Olivia had expected. But something was missing.

"Smile!" she called out. "This is a cheer, not a eulogy!"

Seven smiles immediately appeared on seven faces. They looked pasted on, but fake smiles were better than grim frowns.

"Who's best,
Who's tops,
Who's number one. . . ."

They swung their pompons gracefully until they came to the word *tops*. Then everyone hesitated. It was a reflex action — tops was when Rob and Sean had tangled the day before. And secretly, everyone wondered if it was going to happen again.

Olivia had hesitated with the rest of them, but she decided to pretend they'd all just goofed. "Let's take it again," she directed. "From 'best.' "

This time, nobody missed a beat. No pompons tangled, no tempers flared, no one pushed anyone else. Olivia didn't realize she'd been holding her breath, but she must have, because when it was over, she puffed out about a gallon of air.

Now for the straddle jump. If they could get through that, they might have a cheer on their hands. A simple cheer, but a decent one.

Olivia didn't waste any time putting her next plan into action. "Okay," she said. "Let's work on our jumps. Guys first. The rest of us'll take a break while you go through them."

She knew Rob would have trouble with the jump, but she didn't want to single him out. She figured if she split them into groups, and pretended that they all needed work, then no one would be tempted to make any snide remarks.

Sipping some water, Olivia looked over the rim of her paper cup at the boys. Sean and Peter leaped beautifully, legs spread, fingers almost touching their toes. That didn't surprise Olivia at all.

Rob wasn't much of a surprise, either. His jump was clumsy, heavy, and not nearly high enough. Sean and Peter didn't need any practice at all; Rob needed about a year.

"Try thinking of yourself as a tightly coiled spring before you jump," Olivia called out casually. "Sort of like a jack-in-the-box. Then just pretend that the lid pops up. It works for me."

With a slight nod, Rob tried again. And again. And again. After about twenty tries, he finally did it. It wasn't even close to perfect, but it was an honest-to-goodness straddle jump. It'll pass, Olivia thought. It'll have to.

Looking around, Olivia saw that the others, except for Tara, were ignoring the minor miracle that had just taken place. She didn't expect them to applaud, but it would have been nice if they'd shown a little team spirit.

"That wasn't bad, Rob," she said. "It needs a little work, but it wasn't bad." No sense giving him a swelled head, she thought. After all, he still had a long, long way to go.

"Not bad?" Rob smiled. "I thought it was pretty good, myself. But thanks, I guess."

If Olivia had been a cat, her hair would have bristled. Just who did this guy think he was, anyway? He'd performed a mediocre straddle jump —which really *was* a miracle, considering the fact that he was about ten steps below mediocre — and he was insulted because nobody clapped.

Olivia took a deep breath. "You're welcome, I guess," she said, trying to keep her tone light. "Okay, it's our turn now," she said to the girls. Then she immediately did a jump that was so high, so perfect, and so effortless, that she seemed immune to gravity. Short of punching Rob in the stomach, it was her best revenge.

She was relieved when Mrs. Engborg arrived and took charge.

Half an hour before practice was over, when the cheerleaders were taking a break, Hope walked nervously over to where the coach was sitting.

Maybe she won't mind too much, Hope thought. After all, we've done good work today. Even Rob looks better — a little better — and she has to be happy about that.

"Mrs. Engborg?"

"Yes, Hope."

"I'm sorry, but I'm afraid I'm going to have to leave now," Hope said.

Looking up quickly from her notes, Ardith Engborg frowned. "Are you sick?"

"No, I'm fine," Hope told her. "It's just that I didn't expect extra practice today, and I wasn't able to make any arrangements about my job. About being late for it, I mean."

Mrs. Engborg's frown deepened. "I didn't know you were working. It's all right, of course, but you do know that practice is supposed to come first."

Hope nodded. "It's just that I didn't expect to have extra practice. I'm sorry."

"Well, I suppose there's nothing we can do about it now," Ardith said. "You can go, Hope, but please don't let this happen again. The squad has a lot of work to do. No one can afford to miss practice."

"It won't happen again," Hope assured her. "Thank you, Mrs. Engborg."

Turning away, Hope walked quickly across the gym, anxious to get out. Her eyes were on the big wall clock, calculating to the split second exactly how much time she had, so she didn't see Peter until she bumped into him.

Off balance, the two cheerleaders grabbed at each other to keep from falling. Then they jumped quickly apart, as if they weren't supposed to be touching.

"Sorry," Peter said, wishing she would have kept her arms around him a little longer. "Hope, I — "

"I'm sorry, Peter," Hope broke in. "It was my fault."

"It was?" Was she talking about them, he wondered?

"Yes, I wasn't looking where I was going." Glancing at the clock again, Hope's eyes widened in panic. "Excuse me," she said, edging around him, "I have to hurry. I'll be late for work!"

"Oh. Sure," Peter said, feeling disappointed. "Take it easy, okay?" But Hope, already at the gym doors, didn't hear him.

There won't be time to shower, Hope thought, as she rushed into the locker room and started stripping off her sweaty warm-up clothes. There may not even be time to grab a hot dog. A dirty, hungry salesperson, that's what Mrs. Randolph's going to get.

Grimacing, Hope threw on her clean clothes, stuffed the others into her canvas bag, grabbed her coat, and dashed out of the locker room. She had exactly five minutes to make it to the bus stop, which was a five-minute walk away.

Slinging her bag over her shoulder, Hope began to run, the slap of her boots echoing down the empty tiled hall. Throwing open the door, she hurried down the steps, skidded on the icy sidewalk, kept her balance, and raced across the street, just in front of a large white garbage truck.

Patrick Henley, driving the garbage truck, tapped his window and waved, but Hope Chang didn't even turn her head.

Wonder where the fire is? Patrick thought to himself. He glanced at the high school door, expecting to see some of the other cheerleaders come out. When they didn't, he checked his watch. Twelve o'clock. They were usually out by eleven-thirty, so they must be practicing overtime. Remembering Hope's job, he realized why she'd been in such a hurry.

Now that he had everything figured out, Patrick put the truck into gear, and started to drive on. But when he reached the end of the block, instead of turning right, which was the direction his route took him, he turned left. Then left again, and again, until he was back at the side door of Tarenton High.

During that slow turn around the block, Patrick had done some quick thinking. It was lunch time and he was hungry. He had a sandwich, a bag of corn chips, and an apple with him, so why not eat now?

Second, he wanted to talk to Jessica. Not only did he want to talk to her, he *had* to talk to her. If he didn't, he was going to explode. And since she was inside the high school, why not eat his lunch and bide his time until she came out?

Easing the truck over to the curb, Patrick pulled a turkey sandwich out of his brown paper sack, took a bite, and sat back to wait.

Twenty minutes, a sandwich, and half a bag of corn chips later, the cheerleaders began to emerge. Sean Dubrow came out first, head down, moving fast toward his flashy red car. The guy's got something on his mind, Patrick thought, and whatever it is, it's not good.

Next came Olivia, looking like she'd just been through the wringer. Patrick figured Mrs. Engborg must be working them really hard. Olivia looked around, obviously waiting for someone. Then her arm shot up in the air, and Patrick saw that she was waving to Walt Manners. Walt loped across the parking lot toward Olivia, a big smile on his friendly face. Strange, Patrick thought. He'd been sure that the thing between David Duffy and Olivia was going to last a long time.

Love's a guessing game, he told himself, as he watched Tara Armstrong and Rob Ladd walk through the door together. Those two were a very strange combination. Well, not strange, exactly. But it did seem weird that Tara would decide to pair off with Ladd, considering the fact that the guy was ruining the squad.

Then Patrick stopped wondering about everyone else. Because stepping through the doorway, her brown hair blowing in the wind, was the only one he really cared about — Jessica Bennett. It's now or never, he told himself, and sounded the horn.

The garbage truck's horn filled the air like the bellow of a hungry elephant, and Jessica stopped in her tracks, looking for the source of the racket.

Once he had her attention, Patrick opened the door and stood on the running board. He waved once, gesturing for her to come over, then waited to see what she would do.

Jessica hesitated only a second. Then she took a deep breath and began walking slowly toward Patrick's truck. On her face was the same look Olivia had noticed earlier at practice — a frightened expression, as if she were stepping into the unknown.

CHAPTER

18

Olivia had been right about Tara. She *was* still upset about the things Olivia had said. Playing games with Sean and Rob? Crossing the parking lot with Rob Ladd, Tara tossed her red hair back indignantly. The guys were the ones playing games, not her. She was just watching. All right, so she wasn't a completely objective observer. She was curious to see what would happen between those two, but there was absolutely nothing wrong with that, was there?

"I think," Rob said, breaking into her thoughts, "that we're going to see some changes on the squad pretty soon."

"Oh, I'm sure we will," Tara agreed. "You looked good today, Rob."

"Mmm." Rob nodded and gave her a quick

smile. "Thanks. Our captain didn't seem over-whelmed."

That's for sure, Tara thought. "Oh, well, that's because Olivia's so good, you know. I mean, leaping around and turning herself into a human pretzel just comes naturally to her. She doesn't realize how hard the rest of us have to work at it."

Which wasn't quite true, and Tara knew it. Olivia might have been naturally gifted, but she was always working to perfect that gift. But Tara wasn't in the mood to give Olivia much credit for anything at the moment.

"And she's the captain, too," she went on. "Personally, I don't think it would hurt if she took that job a little less seriously, but what can you do?"

Rob took out his car keys, jiggling them in his hand for a moment. "Well, like I said, I think some changes are in order."

"Oh, right. You'll see, once we're all working well together, Olivia's attitude won't bother you a bit."

"It doesn't bother me now." Rob laughed softly. "I think you and I are talking about two different things."

Tara frowned. Had she really missed something or was he being sarcastic?

"Hey, don't look like that," Rob said. Still laughing, he reached out a finger and brushed it across her forehead, smoothing the frown away. "You look much better when you smile."

Finally, Tara thought, he's touched me again. She'd started to wonder if the time he held her hand that night at Freddy's was going to be the last. Of course, a fingertip on her forehead wasn't exactly a kiss, but it was better than nothing. Tara was sure a kiss couldn't be much longer in coming, and the thought of what it was going to be like brought a smile to her lips.

"That's better," Rob said. "That smile's going to take you a long way, remember that."

"I'll try," Tara said softly, wondering if he was going to kiss her now.

But he wasn't. He simply traced her lips with his cool finger, and then proceeded to open the door of his car. "See you tomorrow morning, Tara. And tomorrow afternoon, right?"

"Oh." Tara mentally shook away her disappointment. "Of course — your party. Yes, I'll be there, Rob."

"Good." With an offhand wave, Rob got in the car, started it, and chugged away, leaving Tara alone in the nearly empty parking lot.

Well, there's no reason to be insulted, Tara told herself. After all, he didn't know you don't have a ride. Not that you need one, since you only live three blocks away. It would have been nice if he'd asked, but he's probably got a thousand things to do for tomorrow. After all, this isn't just a party for a bunch of high school kids. It's the Ladd family's annual holiday buffet. There'll probably be lots of important people there. Maybe even some cute young political aides.

That thought brought another smile to Tara's face, and she hurried up the snowy incline to the sidewalk and headed home, trying to decide what to wear the next day.

If everything had gone as planned, Hope would have reached Langston's exactly twenty-two minutes past the time she was supposed to get there. Twenty-two minutes, she kept thinking, as the bus lurched down the street. How angry can Mrs. Randolph possibly get over a measly twenty-two minutes?

She'd almost convinced herself that underneath Mrs. Randolph's frozen exterior beat a warm, understanding heart, when she suddenly realized that things were not going to go as planned.

The bus, pulling away from the curb, lurched again. And then again. They weren't the usual lurches, either. These were the kind of bucking, trembling lurches that spelled trouble. Mechanical trouble.

"Sit tight, folks," the driver said, getting out of his seat. "I'll just go have a look and see what's happened."

Hope closed her eyes and crossed her fingers. Please, she thought, don't let it be anything bad. Let it be something easy to fix. Easy and fast.

The driver was back. "Sorry, folks," he said, "it's axle trouble. I'll radio for a backup, but make yourselves comfortable. Looks like we'll be here for a while."

Hope opened her eyes, uncrossed her fingers,

and made her way up to the driver's seat. "Excuse me," she said. "But do you have any idea how long this might take?"

The driver shook his head. "Can't say for sure. I'd guess . . . oh, forty-five minutes."

Forty-five minutes. Mrs. Randolph's heart might be understanding about twenty-two minutes, but forty-five more? Hope's own heart sank.

"I'm afraid I can't wait that long," she told the driver. "I'm late for work at the mall. I can get there faster walking."

"I won't argue with that," the driver said jovially, opening the door. "Watch yourself though, there aren't any sidewalks around here and the traffic gets pretty thick."

Hope thanked him, wishing *he* were her boss, and got off the bus. She wasn't sure how far the mall was, maybe a mile. A mile wasn't so bad, she thought. At a brisk pace a mile should only take a few minutes.

But Hope hadn't counted on the snowbanks. The streets were clear, but they were also full of cars and trucks, and since there were no sidewalks, she had to walk as far to the side as possible. And the sides were piled with banks of snow as high as three feet, where the snowplows had shoved them. Some of the mounds were thick and crusty, and Hope was able to walk without sinking. But not for long. Every once in a while, she'd take a step and find herself in snow up to her kneecaps.

After her fifth soft snowbank, Hope was beginning to think she should have stayed on the bus. Her boots were getting ruined, her feet were freezing, and she was already forty minutes late for work.

That's when she saw the red car zip past, slow down, and then do a quick U-turn, pulling up as close as possible to where she was struggling to free her leg from a foot of filthy snow.

In a second, Sean Dubrow was at her side. He took her hand in a strong grip, pulled her free of the snow, hurried her into his car, and drove off.

"Where you headed?" he asked, as if there was nothing unusual about the situation.

"Langston's," Hope said, pulling off her gloves and blowing on her fingers.

Another U-turn, and the red Fiero was heading in the right direction.

"Thank you, Sean," Hope said. "I was beginning to feel like a mountain climber."

"That's what you looked like," Sean said with a grin. "You may have just discovered a new sport: climbing the snowbanks of Tarenton."

They both laughed. "Well," Hope told him, "you saved my life, but I don't know about my job."

"Oh, right. That's why you had to leave practice early."

"Yes. And then the bus broke down and I decided it would be faster to walk." Hope checked her watch. "It looks like I was wrong."

"I'll get you there as fast as legally possible," Sean told her, pressing down slightly on the gas pedal.

"What about those two U-turns?" Hope asked with a smile. "Those weren't legal, were they?"

"Sure they were! They were part of a rescue operation."

Laughing, Hope settled back into the soft bucket seat.

"Tell me something," Sean asked. "Why were you knocking yourself out like that? I mean, if it had been me, I would have stuck with the bus, or gotten to a pay phone and told my boss I'd be late — take it or leave it."

Yes, that's just what Sean would do, Hope thought. But I couldn't. Why? "Well, I was late before I even got on the bus," she explained. "And when the axle broke, or whatever it was, I guess I just panicked."

Sean glanced over at Hope, surprise in his dark eyes. "You? You're not the panicky kind."

"What do you mean?"

"I'm not sure." Shrugging, Sean pulled the car smoothly into the mall's parking lot and stopped right in front of the entrance to Langston's. "I guess I mean that you've got a lot of pride, or guts, or whatever. People like you don't panic."

Hope was embarrassed and pleased at the same time. Sean Dubrow had never paid her a compliment that she could remember, and it felt good.

"Well, anyway," Sean went on. "Here we are."

"Thank you," Hope said again, getting out of the car.

"Any time," he told her. "And listen, tell that boss of yours what happened. If she doesn't like it, tough." With a roar, the Fiero took off, and Hope, her boots squishing with melted snow, hurried into the store.

"Miss Chang." Mrs. Randolph was waiting behind the counter, her eyes colder than ever. "You're forty-five minutes late. I hope you have an explanation."

"Yes, I do," Hope said. "Didn't you get my message?"

"Message?"

Hope nodded. "I called this morning and said I'd be twenty minutes late. I'm not sure who took the message, but she said you'd get it."

"Well, I didn't." Mrs. Randolph's expression didn't change. "But even if I had, that doesn't explain the extra twenty-five minutes. Would you care to explain it?"

"The bus broke down," Hope said, unbuttoning her coat. "I walked part of the way and then a friend picked me up in his car. I'm sorry I'm late, but I got here as fast as I could."

It was so obviously the truth, that Mrs. Randolph couldn't argue. Hope decided there was nothing more to say. Stuffing her duffel bag and coat under the counter, she walked over to the scarf table and started folding.

But Mrs. Randolph followed her, and when

Hope glanced up, she said, "It's just as well that you *were* late, I suppose. We're absolutely overwhelmed with returns, and since we still haven't found a replacement for that irresponsible girl who quit at the height of the season, you can make up the time by working an extra shift."

Hope stopped folding. "Mrs. Randolph," she said, "I've worked an extra shift for three days. I even worked an extra shift on Christmas Eve. I can't do it today."

"But you were late."

"That wasn't my fault."

Mrs. Randolph was close to sputtering. "Nevertheless, I'm asking you to work late today."

Hope put down the scarf she was holding. She smiled politely, and her voice was calm, but her shoulders were back and her dark eyes were serious. "I'm sorry," she said. "I can't."

"All right," Patrick said, keeping his voice even. "It's time we talked."

"You're right," Jessica agreed. "It *is* time."

"Now, all I want you to do right now is listen, okay?" Patrick said. "I've been doing a lot of thinking, and a lot of this may come out all jumbled up, so just let me talk. Okay?"

Jessica nodded. They'd been sitting sliently in the garbage truck for almost half an hour, while Patrick made his rounds. He had to get them out of the way, he said, and then they'd talk. Now he was on a break, and it was time. "Go ahead," she told him. "I'll listen."

"Good." Patrick thought for a second, and then spoke quickly, his words tumbling out in a rush. "I have two things I want to say, and then you can go, if you want to. The first is, I think I finally figured out what's holding you back. You're scared."

Jessica started to say something, but Patrick held up his hand.

"Let me finish. I know, you're going to accuse Pres of talking behind your back. Well, he did. But he only did it because he's my friend, so don't get mad at him. It's getting cold in this crate," Patrick said suddenly. He started the truck, turned on the heater, and drove slowly down the street.

"Like I said," he went on after a minute, "I think you're scared." When Jessica didn't answer, he shook his head. "Boy, that's the last thing I expected of you, Jessica. If anybody had ever told me that Jessica Bennett was a chicken, I would have laughed in their face. But now I'm not so sure."

Jessica couldn't keep quiet any longer. "You don't know what you're talking about!" she cried angrily. "You don't understand!"

"That's right, I don't!" Patrick said just as angrily. "And I'm not letting you out of this noisy, bumpy truck until you tell me!"

Pulling the truck over to the curb again, Patrick turned the engine off and faced Jessica. "Would you please tell me?" he said more quietly.

211

Jessica took a shaky breath. "I was going to tell you," she said. "I was up late last night just thinking about it." Another shaky breath. "I didn't mean to yell at you just now. You're right, I *am* scared. Patrick, this is going to sound silly, but I'm just afraid of getting hurt. I lost my father and I know this is different, but still, I just don't think I could bear getting close to somebody and then losing him, too."

Patrick stared at her, and slowly, a smile spread across his face. "You mean me?"

"Who else?" Jessica asked. "Didn't Pres tell you what else I said — that if I *did* want to get involved with anyone, it would be you?"

"Sure he did," Patrick told her. "That was the kick I needed to come and talk to you."

"Well, then," Jessica said. "What do we do now?"

Still smiling, Patrick slid across the seat until he was close to her. "I have the perfect plan," he said softly. "We get involved."

Without waiting for her answer, he began to kiss her, slowly and gently, then more and more strongly until Jessica realized that her arms were around his neck and she was kissing him back.

"I'm . . . I'm still scared, Patrick," she whispered against his cheek.

"I know that," he said. "And I'm not sure what to say except that you're right, this is different. I'm *not* your father. And I can't make any promises, but I'm pretty sure I'm not going to die on you." He kissed the top of her head, then touched his lips to her eyes. "Sometimes, if you want something bad enough, you just have to take a chance."

"I know." Jessica put the tips of her fingers on Patrick's lips and smiled. "So this is what it feels like to jump into the deep end."

"What?"

"I always thought of falling in love as jumping into the deep end of a swimming pool."

"Well, can you swim?" Patrick asked with a laugh.

"I can try."

"I'll help," he told her. "After all, I'll be right there with you. I know what I want, Jessica, and I'm going to take a chance."

Tightening her arms, Jessica pulled him closer. "I know what I want, too," she said softly. Before she kissed him, she whispered, "I want you."

CHAPTER

That night, just after Patrick dropped Jessica off at her house, the clouds opened and began dropping fat flakes of snow on Tarenton. They fell slowly at first, but then the wind picked up, the temperature dropped, and the snow fell faster until people realized that they had a full-fledged storm on their hands.

Patrick, still in an ecstatic daze, hardly noticed it even though he was driving through it, and Jessica didn't notice it at all. She simply floated into her house, into her room, and dropped onto her bed. Then she stared at the ceiling, a dreamy smile on her face, until she finally fell asleep.

Olivia, watching from her bedroom window, hoped that enough snow would fall to keep Walt's plane grounded. He was leaving tomorrow, and once he left, Olivia knew she'd be on her own. No more Walt to help her escape from her problems.

In her bedroom, Tara kept hoping the snow *would* stop. If it didn't, Rob might have to cancel his party tomorrow. She'd spent too much time and energy thinking about it, deciding what to wear, and wondering whether anything exciting was going to happen, to give it up now.

Peter saw the snow and wished it would go on for days, burying the town under a blanket so deep that nobody would be able to go anywhere. Especially Hope. Maybe if she was away from that job long enough, she'd realize how much it had changed her.

Hope completely ignored the storm. She played Scrabble with James, and then she practiced her violin for an hour and a half.

After pulling his car into the garage, Sean dashed back into his house, popped himself some popcorn, opened a soda, and sat back on the couch to watch a football game. The picture was rotten, though, almost as snowy as the view from the living room window, so he finally snapped off the set.

It was a nice little speech he'd made to Hope today, about being proud and having guts. He'd always thought *he* wasn't the panicky kind, either. But as he sat in the darkened room and watched the storm swirl outside, he had to admit that it would be very nice if Ladd had to cancel his annual family buffet.

By nine-thirty the next morning, the storm had

blown itself out, leaving eight inches of new snow on the ground. The plows, busy all night on the main roads, began to tackle the rest of the town. People emerged from their houses and started digging out their cars, and by noon, traffic was almost back to normal. The sun came out strong, and Walt's plane lifted into the sky only twenty minutes behind schedule. Rob Ladd's party went ahead as planned, and the only thing canceled was cheerleading practice.

At three-thirty that afternoon, Tara, wearing a wrap-around skirt of soft blue wool, a silk paisley blouse, a navy blue coat, and navy blue leather boots, got out of her father's car and walked up the shoveled stone path to the Ladd house.

The house was stone, too, three stories high, with dark green shutters and lots of windows. It was set back from the street, half-hidden by five immense evergreen trees. The massive wooden front door had a brass knocker in the shape of a snarling lion, but it also had a doorbell, which Tara pushed.

A uniformed maid opened the door, took Tara's coat, and directed her down a wide hallway toward a set of French doors. Tara paused just a second in front of an oval mirror in the hall to check her hair, and then went in.

The room was huge. It must have run almost the entire width of the house, and the back wall was all windows, looking out on a large snowy yard. At one end of the room was a stone fireplace with a roaring fire, and at the other end was a long table covered with white linen and platters of food.

In spite of its size, the room had a comfortable, lived-in feel to it. The oriental rugs were slightly worn in places, the chairs were deep and soft, and the high oak shelves were crammed full of well-thumbed books.

About fifty people were milling around, chatting and eating, but Tara didn't see Rob at first, or anyone else she knew, except for Judson Abbott. He was talking to a tall, slender woman in a red wool dress. The woman had pale brown hair and a thin mouth that curved in a half-smile as she listened to Abbott. Rob's mother, Tara thought. She was wondering whether she should go over and introduce herself, when a voice said, "I recommend the shrimp."

Turning, Tara found herself facing Sean Dubrow, who looked extremely handsome in a chocolate brown sports jacket and dark red tie. "Sean!" she said, "I didn't think you'd . . . . I mean. . . ."

Sean's dark eyes sparkled. "Go ahead, Tara. Finish it."

"Well," Tara said, tossing her hair back from her face, "you know what I mean. I didn't think you'd want to come, considering the way you feel about our host."

"You're right, I didn't want to come," Sean admitted. "But I said I'd be here and here I am." It had taken Sean a good hour to talk himself into coming. He'd finally decided to put in an appearance, just to keep from giving Rob the satisfaction of asking why he didn't show up. "Anyway, like I said," he went on, "the shrimp's terrific. And I haven't seen our gracious 'host' since I got here, so things aren't all bad."

"Would you keep your voice down?" Tara hissed. "Somebody might hear. This is his house, you know."

Sean nodded. "Yep. It's perfect, too. Made out of rocks." Leaning closer, he whispered, "The same rocks Rob crawled out from under, I'll bet."

Shaking her head, Tara moved away toward the buffet table and took a plate. Not only were there shrimp — enormous shrimp on a bed of cracked ice — but there was cold crab, too. Plus a roast turkey, stuffed mushrooms, French bread, cheeses, and about ten different kinds of salads. Tara ignored the shrimp, and took a little of everything else.

The room was filled with laughter and talk, and as she turned from the table, Tara heard Jessica's voice. Craning her neck, she spotted her fellow cheerleader over by the fireplace with Patrick Henley and Peter Rayman.

Tara really didn't want to hang out with just cheerleaders, but since she didn't know anyone else in the room, she didn't have much choice. She certainly didn't want to talk to Sean at the moment. Wondering where Rob was, she made her way across the room to the fireplace.

"Hi!" she said when she reached the others. "Isn't this great?"

"The food is," Peter said, glancing at his watch. "Half an hour more. Do you think that's long enough to stay?"

Jessica laughed. "I was thinking more like fifteen minutes."

Patrick shook his head, his arm around Jessica's shoulder. "Peter's right. Half an hour. Then nobody can accuse us of being rude."

"I don't get it," Tara said. "Why do you want to leave so fast?"

"Because we don't belong here," Jessica explained.

"Why not? Rob invited us."

"That's the reason we want to leave," Peter said.

"Oh, honestly!" Tara sighed. "Are you going to act like this forever? I mean, he's on the squad now, whether we like it or not, and he's getting much better."

Peter and Jessica stared at her like she was crazy, and Tara blushed. Rob wasn't getting *much* better, even she had to admit that. "Well, he's getting a little better," she said.

Jessica couldn't believe it. Had Tara really forgotten exactly how Rob got on the squad? She wanted to ask, but with Patrick there, she couldn't get into it. Instead, she took Patrick's hand, lifted it so she could see his watch, and made an obvious point of checking the time.

Tara sighed again, and went over to say hi to Olivia, who'd just come into the room.

Smiling, Patrick leaned over and kissed Jessica softly on the cheek. "I'm with you," he whispered. "The sooner we can get out of here, the sooner we can be alone."

Next to them, Peter shifted uncomfortably, twisting his neck and wishing he hadn't worn a tie. He hated ties; they were the most useless piece of clothing ever invented.

But the tie wasn't the only thing making Peter uncomfortable. Jessica and Patrick were having trouble keeping their hands off each other, and he couldn't help wishing they'd take their happiness somewhere else. It only reminded him of what he was missing, not that he needed any reminders.

At that moment, Jessica burst out laughing at something Patrick said, and across the room, Tara poked Olivia in the ribs. "Look at them," she said. "You'd think they were the only two people in the room."

"Mmm." Olivia smiled. Whatever had been bothering Jessica yesterday sure wasn't bothering her today. She was glowing like a light bulb. So was Patrick, for that matter. Good, Olivia thought. She liked Patrick, and if Jessica could make him light up like that, then good for Jessica. "Well," she said in a low voice, "at least somebody's having a good time."

"Oh, not you, too," Tara remarked. "Honestly, everybody's complaining like crazy about being here. No one twisted your arms to come, you know."

"I know," Olivia admitted. "I'm just not in the mood for a party. Anyway, where's Rob?"

"I haven't seen him," Tara reported. "But Sean's here."

Looking around, Olivia spotted Sean stabbing up shrimp with a toothpick and waved to him. Sean waved back, finished filling his plate, and started across the room toward Olivia.

That was when Rob Ladd made his entrance. He breezed through the French doors, his eyes on Judson Abbott, who was on the opposite side of the room, and bumped solidly into Sean Dubrow.

All eyes followed Sean's plate. It sailed up and out of his hands, made a lazy flip in midair, and fell with a thud onto the rug. The shrimp followed the same arc, plopping softly at Sean's feet.

"Well, well, Dubrow!" Rob said with a smile. "I see you're enjoying the food."

Everyone laughed, and Sean forced himself to join in.

"Be with you in a minute," Rob said to the room in general, and hurried over to Judson Abbott.

The chatter resumed its normal level; everyone seemed to have forgotten that there were half a dozen shrimp and a splotch of coctkail sauce on the floor. Sean couldn't forget, though — some of the sauce was on his pants.

Slowly, he knelt down, retrieved his plate, and started picking the shrimp off the rug.

"Don't feel bad," Olivia said, coming over to help him. "Once I spilled an entire jar of pickles on somebody's floor, and every time I pass the house, I think I can still smell pickle juice."

Sean nodded, but he didn't laugh, and the two of them cleaned up the mess in silence.

Peter, feeling embarrassed for Sean, too, started across the room to help, but halfway there, he stopped, staring.

Standing in the doorway was a girl wearing dark red velvet pants and a lacy white blouse. She had almond-shaped eyes, satiny dark hair, and a smile on her face. It was Hope, and she was smiling at Peter.

Peter forgot about everything but the girl in the doorway, and barely missed crushing a shrimp into the rug as he walked over to her.

"Hi," Hope said when he reached her.

"Hi." Peter looked confused. "What are you doing here? I thought you had to work."

"I know. I thought so, too." Laughing, Hope looked around the crowded room. "Do you think we could find someplace to talk?"

Peter stuck his head out the door and checked the hall. Empty, except for the maid who'd taken his coat. But she was up by the front door, and the hall was plenty long. "Come on," he said. "Let's go out here."

Around the door they found a long wooden bench. They both sat down, and Peter turned to Hope. "So. Why aren't you at work?"

Hope jumped up, a funny smile on her face. Taking a deep breath, she said, "I got fired."

"You what?"

"Fired," Hope said again. "I am no longer part of the 'Happy Langston Family of Employees.' "

Peter was shocked. Hope was the most responsible girl he knew; she always gave a hundred percent to anything she did. He noticed that Hope didn't look broken up about it, so he tried a joke. "I guess they caught you, huh?"

"Caught me?"

Peter shook his head, pretending to be serious. "I should have warned you. Embezzling's a serious offense."

Laughing again, Hope described what had happened the day before with the bus. "So when Mrs. Randolph told me that I'd have to work late," she finished, "something inside me just clicked. And I told her I couldn't. It wasn't fair for her to ask me, and she knew it. She was trying to get back at me, and I just couldn't let her do it."

"But you can't be fired for that!" Now Peter was indignant. "I mean, you were hired to work certain hours. They can't force you to work overtime."

"Oh, she didn't fire me for that," Hope told him. "She fired me for being late. That's what she said, anyway."

"But it wasn't your fault," Peter protested.

"Peter, it doesn't matter." Hope sat down

again, fingering the beautiful bracelet he'd given her for Christmas. "I was glad it happened, really."

Noticing the bracelet, Peter smiled. Hope saw the smile, and took his hand. "You were right," she said. "I should never have taken that job. I guess I was trying to be somebody I'm not. More . . . I don't know. . . . More outgoing and friendly and busy. You know, like everybody else."

Peter nodded, tightening his grip on her hand.

"I thought I was dull," Hope went on. "In a rut. So serious about my music and things." She sighed and shook her head. "But that's who I am, I guess."

"That's not true," Peter argued. "There aren't many girls — or guys, either — who get straight A's, and play the violin like a master, and belong to the Varsity Squad, and whip everybody at Scrabble. and . . . you want me to go on?"

Hope was blushing. "No," she said, "I think I get the idea. And I'm sorry I acted the way I did. I guess I just had to find out for myself."

"I can understand that." Peter kissed her softly, and grinned. "So you're not mad at anybody anymore, huh?"

"Oh. that reminds, me!" Hope laughed again. "My parents are crazy about you now."

"They are? No kidding!"

"Yes, my mother said that once they realized how much you cared about me, they felt ashamed that they'd ever tried to keep us apart."

"Amazing," Peter said. "They're right, you know. And Hope?"

"Yes?"

"I wouldn't care about you half as much if you weren't so . . . 'dull.' I love you just the way you are."

As Peter bent to kiss her again, there was a loud burst of laughter from the other room, but neither of them heard it at all.

CHAPTER

"I wonder what happened to Peter and Hope," Olivia said, looking around.

"They're having a very heavy conversation out in the hall," Tara reported. "I just looked. I didn't hear what they were saying, but it sounded serious."

"Happy-serious or sad-serious?"

Tara shrugged. She wasn't interested in Peter and Hope at the moment. She was beginning to wonder when Rob was going to pay some attention to her. So far, he'd spent his entire time talking to Judson Abbott, and that conversation looked serious, too, so Tara didn't think she should join in.

Normally, Tara could have found dozens of people to talk to. But she didn't know any of these people, except for the other cheerleaders.

She'd had visions of a lot of young, handsome unattached politicians being here, but it hadn't turned out that way at all. The young handsome guys were very definitely attached — to young pretty women. And the others were all over forty. She wasn't even sure if any of them were politicians, except for Judson Abbott. For all she knew, they could have been neighbors and relatives.

This party was not turning out the way Tara had hoped. She checked her watch, just like the others did, to see how soon she could leave without being rude. Still too soon to go.

Restlessly, she moved over to the food table. She wasn't hungry; she'd already eaten enough salad to turn her green, but at least it gave her something to do.

She was standing there, trying to choose between the Caesar and the sprout, when she felt a hand on her shoulder.

"Sorry I left you alone so long," Rob said. "My father had a lot of messages for me to give Judd."

"Oh, well, that's all right," Tara told him, feeling better already. "I was wondering where your father was. I thought he'd be home for the holidays."

"He was, for Christmas anyway. But he had to fly back to the capitol for a meeting," Rob explained. "He was supposed to be here today, but the storm just hit out there and he couldn't make it back."

"That's too bad."

"Yeah, well, we'll just have to make do without him," Rob said. "Anyway, how're you doing?"

"Fine."

"Oh?" Rob raised an eyebrow. "I'm a little bored, myself. I go through this every year and it never fails — I start to nod out about five o'clock."

Then why did you invite us? Tara felt like asking.

But Rob didn't notice the way Tara was looking at him. His eyes were on Sean, who was inspecting the books and trying to stifle a yawn. "Dubrow looks bored, that's for sure," he said, chuckling quietly. "Poor guy. Well, at least he's up front about it, I'll give him that much."

"What do you mean, 'poor guy'?" Tara asked.

"I mean he doesn't fit in," Rob said, putting his arm around her shoulder. "You do. The rest of the squad does. But not Dubrow." Tightening his grip on her, he leaned close. "You remember when I talked about changes on the squad?" he asked.

Tara nodded.

"Well," Rob said softly, "I'll let you in on a secret. I was talking about Dubrow. He doesn't fit in here, and I'm beginning to think he doesn't quite fit in with the new squad, either."

Tara couldn't believe what she was hearing. Was Rob actually suggesting that Sean Dubrow shouldn't be on the squad? She stared at Rob, her eyes wide.

Rob laughed and pulled her closer to him.

"Hey, don't tell me you're surprised." His fingers moved up, caressing her neck. "Come on, Tara. We're two of a kind. You're on my side, aren't you?"

Tara was still trying to decide if he was serious or joking. He always had that semi-smile on his face, and it was impossible to tell. If it was a joke, she thought, it wasn't a very funny one. And if he was serious, then she didn't want any part of him. She thought she knew him, but now she realized he was a complete mystery.

"Rob, dear," a soft, mellow voice said, "I'm afraid you're being a very bad host."

Mrs. Ladd, a thin smile on her face, had suddenly appeared at the food table. "Here you are, monopolizing this young girl's attention, and you haven't even introduced me to her. Or to any of the other cheerleaders, I might add."

"You're right, Mother," Rob said smoothly. "But you can't blame me for spending so much time with Tara Armstrong."

Putting down her plate, Tara shrugged away from Rob, and shook hands with his mother.

"Now that you've met Tara," Rob went on, "I should introduce you to the rest of the squad." Raising his voice, he called the rest of the cheerleaders over. Hope and Peter had just reentered the room, hand-in-hand, and they joined Sean, Olivia, and Jessica.

One by one, Rob gave their names. When he got to Sean, he grinned. "And this," he said, clapping Sean on the shoulder as if they were the best of buddies, "is Sean Dubrow. He's quite a cheerleader, and quite a ladies' man, too."

Sean shook hands with Mrs. Ladd, and started to turn away. But Rob wasn't finished. "Yes," he said, "Dubrow is very fast on his feet. On the squad, that is. Off the squad, well, that's another story."

Bending down, Rob picked a piece of crushed shrimp from the rug and held it up for everyone to see. "Now most of you wouldn't think that this was the handiwork of a guy who was fast on his feet, would you? Well, it just goes to show you, nobody's perfect. Right, Dubrow?"

Rob said all this with a good-natured smile, his hand still on Sean's shoulder. Most people laughed because they thought he was just kidding around with a good friend. They didn't know what Tara knew — that Rob was out to get Sean any way he could.

Sean handled it pretty well, considering Rob had just humiliated him in front of a roomful of people. Laughing with the rest of them, he backed away and aimed a playful punch at Rob's arm. Then he turned, still laughing, and walked over to the fireplace.

Tara watched him, wishing the punch he'd given Rob hadn't been playful at all. Rob deserves a lot more than a tap on the arm, she thought. He deserves a good thump on the head. She was just about to go over to Sean and tell him so, when Olivia gasped.

"Oh, my gosh," Olivia said in a low voice. "I don't believe it!"

Distracted from Sean, Tara turned to see what Olivia was talking about.

There in the doorway stood David Duffy.

Olivia really couldn't believe it. What was he doing here? He wasn't invited, was he? No, she was sure he wasn't. And after what Mrs. Engborg had told her about Judson Abbott's reaction to David, she was sure he wouldn't be welcome, either.

He certainly looked like he belonged, though. Hatless for once, David was dressed in dark slacks, a beige sports jacket, and a blue shirt that matched his eyes. He was even wearing regular shoes instead of his scruffy sneakers. He fit right in, smiling around as if he weren't a total stranger to ninety-five percent of the people in the room.

David might not have been welcome, but he quickly made himself at home, heading straight for the food table. Olivia, recovering from the shock of seeing him, decided she'd better find out what was going on.

She edged in beside him, picked up a plate for herself, and whispered, "What are you doing here?"

"Helping myself to some turkey, at the moment," David whispered back. His eyes were sparkling. "It looks great. How're the mushrooms?"

"I haven't eaten anything yet," Olivia said, taking some meatballs. "And you haven't answered my question."

"Oh, right — what am I doing here? My job, that's what."

"I knew it!" Olivia chewed furiously on a meatball. "David, you've got to get out. If Judson Abbott sees you, he'll freak."

"Not if we just keep our backs to him," David said. "I blend in pretty well, don't you think? As long as he doesn't see my face, he'll think I'm just another political aide or a lobbyist or something."

"David, you weren't invited," Olivia reminded him. "You're not supposed to be here."

"True, but what reporter was ever stopped from following a lead just because he didn't have an invitation?" Reaching out, he brushed Olivia's hair off her forehead and laughed softly. "Come on, Olivia, don't look so worried. If I get caught, I'll take the rap. No problem."

Olivia sighed. "I don't know what you expect to find out here."

"Ah ha!" David popped a mushroom into his mouth and chewed quickly. "I had a brainstorm," he said, swallowing. "I'm not getting anywhere with Abbott, and I'm not getting anywhere with the squad. So I decided to come straight to the source."

"Rob?"

"Nope. His father," David said. "Where is the senator, anyway? I haven't seen him."

"Well, don't bother looking," Olivia told him. "He's not here. I heard Rob tell Tara that he's stuck at the capitol."

"Rats!" David looked disappointed. "And I went to all the trouble of ironing my shirt, too. What a waste."

"That's right," Olivia agreed. "And since you shouldn't have come in the first place, maybe now you'll go."

"Oh, come on, Olivia." David looked down at his plate, which was filled with food, and then said pleadingly, "I've only had two bites, and this stuff looks terrific. If I have to leave, at least let me leave with a full stomach."

"But what about Judson Abbott?" Olivia asked. "And Rob?"

"No problem," David assured her. "I'll find myself a nice secluded chair in a corner, and you can come stand in front of me while I eat. That way, nobody'll see my face."

"Well, all right," Olivia said reluctantly. "But after you eat, you leave."

While Olivia and David were at the food table, Rob's mother had waylaid Tara and talked to her for five long minutes about how wonderful it was that Rob was on the cheerleading squad now. Tara had listened politely, and said all the right things, but she was itching to get away, and it was all she could do not to look at her watch every thirty seconds.

Finally, Mrs. Ladd spotted someone else she wanted to talk to, and Tara made a beeline for the fireplace.

Sean wasn't there. Tara looked quickly around the room, craning her neck to see past the clumps of people, and finally saw Sean disappearing through the French doors.

Hurrying across the room, Tara rushed out the door and caught up with Sean, just as he was about to get his coat from the maid.

"Sean, don't go yet," she said. "I have to talk to you."

"Can't it wait, Tara?" he asked, barely looking at her.

"No, it can't." Tara put her hand on his arm and gave a little tug. "Please, Sean, it's important."

Seeing the worried expression on her face, Sean finally nodded. "All right," he said. "But we'll have to talk out here. I don't want to go back into that room."

Tara looked up and down the hall. The maid was the only one there right now, but people would start leaving soon, and it wouldn't be very private. Still holding Sean's arm, she pulled him halfway down the hall to another door, and opened it.

The room was empty except for a few chairs and a billiards table. Closing the door behind them, Tara walked over to the table and leaned against it, facing Sean.

Sean kept his hand on the doorknob. "Okay," he said. "What's so important? I hope this doesn't take long, because I'd really like to get out of here."

"I don't blame you," Tara told him. "Rob acted like a real creep before, with that shrimp."

"Yeah, well." Sean shrugged. "It doesn't matter."

"Of course it does!" Tara cried. "Why aren't you steamed about it?"

"Look, Tara, the guy made me feel like an idiot," Sean said. "I'll get steamed later. Right now, I just want to go."

"Okay, but what's going to happen when he makes a fool of you again?" Tara asked. "Because he will, you know. He's out to get you, Sean."

Sean looked skeptical.

"I don't mean 'get' you," Tara explained. "Not like that. But he wants you off the squad. He told me so."

"That's crazy," Sean said. "He can't do that."

"No? I didn't think so, either. But look at you," Tara told him. "You're ready to crawl away because he made you feel like an idiot!"

"This isn't the first time he's done it, Tara."

"And it won't be the last." Tara pushed away from the billiards table and walked over to Sean. "I think he's hoping that you'll get so fed up with him and so down on yourself that you'll quit the squad," she said. "And from the way you're acting today, it looks like it just might work."

235

Sean started to say something, then changed his mind, shrugging again.

"Don't shrug your shoulders at me like that, Sean Dubrow!" Tara was furious. "Don't you dare. You care about the squad and about being a cheerleader, and you know it!"

"Sure, I care!" Sean said, starting to get a little angry at the way she was talking to him. "I wasn't sure *you* did, though. I mean, you practically welcomed Rob with open arms, and the guy's a total klutz. You go out with him, you come to his party, you play up to him every chance you get."

"I was wrong!" Tara cried. "That's one of the things I'm trying to tell you. I was completely wrong." She stopped and put out her hand. "And I'm sorry, Sean. I really am. But don't you be wrong, too."

Ignoring her hand, Sean kept his eyes on Tara's face. "What do you mean?"

"I mean, you can't give in, Sean." Tara grabbed his hand and held it tight. "I used to think you and Rob were exactly alike, except that you've got talent and he couldn't cheer his way out of a paper bag."

Sean smiled. "I can't argue with that."

"But you're not alike at all," Tara went on. "Oh, you're both good-looking and you both know it," she said with a grin. "But you wouldn't ever do anything to anybody like Rob's trying to do to you. You're a decent person, Sean, and he's a — "

"How about something that crawled out from under a rock?" Sean suggested, squeezing her hand.

"That's not bad enough for what he is," Tara said with a laugh. "But anyway, what I'm trying to say is, don't back down. If you don't back down, then he can't push you down. Because you're stronger."

Still holding her hand, Sean pulled her close, put his arm around her, and kissed her. "Thanks, Tara," he said softly. "You were right. I was backing down. But I won't anymore, you can count on it."

"That's all I wanted to hear," Tara told him, and she kissed him back.

"Well, I feel much better," Sean said, his cocky smile back to normal. "What do we do now? Play billiards?"

"Are you kidding?" Stepping around him, Tara opened the door and looked out. "It's all clear," she reported, and held out her hand. "Come on, let's go!"

Hand in hand, they dashed down the hall, retrieved their coats, and stepped out into the cold fresh air, like two prisoners who'd just been set free.

CHAPTER

21

Olivia watched as David swallowed the last bite of turkey and washed it down with the last drop of fruit punch. Wiping his mouth with a napkin, he started to sink back into the chair.

"Oh, no you don't," she said. "You've eaten and now you leave. That was the deal."

"But what about dessert?" David asked.

"There isn't any."

"Really? I was sure I saw about five plates piled with pastry over there." David tried to peer around Olivia, but she shifted so she blocked his view.

"Come on, David," she said. "I'm serious. If Judson Abbott sees you here, you're going to be in trouble." And so's the squad, she thought. If Abbott saw this pushy reporter around, he'd really make things hard for Mrs. Engborg.

"You're just lucky he hasn't spotted you yet. So let's go," she said again.

" 'Let's'? Does that mean you're leaving, too?"

Olivia nodded. "I might as well. The problem is, how are we going to get you out of here without anyone seeing you?"

"I could put my jacket over my head and you could lead me out," David suggested.

Olivia ignored that. Looking around, she saw that Jessica, Patrick, Peter, and Hope were saying their good-byes to Rob and his mother. Catching Patrick's eye, she waved him over, and told him to stand in front of David. Then she went over to Rob and Mrs. Ladd.

"Thanks so much for inviting us," she said. "It was very nice."

"Going so soon, Olivia?" Rob asked.

"I'm afraid so," Olivia told him. "I have to get home and. . . ." Her voice trailed off as she tried to think of something she had to do. But Rob had already turned away and started talking to someone else.

"Come on, you guys," Olivia whispered to the other cheerleaders. "We've got to get David out without anyone seeing him."

"Why?" Jessica asked.

"Because he crashed the party. He wanted to interview Senator Ladd."

"I read his article," Hope whispered to Olivia as the four of them headed for David. "He's really serious about getting to the bottom of this, isn't he?"

Olivia nodded, frowning.

"You can't blame him for that," Peter commented. "It's his job."

"I know," Olivia agreed. "But I wish he'd do his job somewhere else. Like in Timbuktu."

Surrounded by four cheerleaders and Patrick Henley. David made a slow, ungraceful, but well-concealed exit from the room. Once they were out of the house, everyone burst out laughing.

"I still don't understand why we did that," Patrick remarked, "but it was fun. Next time you need a cover-up, David, let me know."

"Thanks," David said. "There may just be a story in this: VARSITY SQUAD SAVES REPORTER'S NECK."

"It's better than REPORTER THROWN OUT OF SENATOR'S HOUSE," Olivia remarked.

"True," David admitted. "Thanks, you guys. Come on, Olivia, I'll take you home."

Once she was in David's car, Olivia let out a sigh of relief. "Am I glad to be out of there!"

"It wasn't the most exciting party I've ever been to," David agreed, pulling away from the curb.

"That's not what I meant," Olivia said. "I still can't believe you showed up there, David. Judson Abbott could make a lot of trouble for you, you know."

"Now that's exactly what I've been wanting to ask you," David told her. "Just how did you know that Abbott wouldn't be happy to see me?"

"Well, I. . . ."

"You're right, of course, he *wouldn't* be happy.

240

In fact, the last thing he said to me before he threw me out of his office was that he never wanted to see my face again. But how did you know, Olivia?"

Olivia swallowed. "Mrs. Engborg told me," she admitted.

"And how did your coach know?" David asked. "She didn't hear it from me, so she must have heard it from Judson Abbott. Am I right?"

Olivia nodded.

David gave a low whistle as he drove down the street. "Now that really makes things interesting. Why would Abbott go running to Ardith Engborg about some pesty reporter?" He whistled again. "It's all beginning to tie in," he said.

"What's beginning to tie in to what?" Olivia wanted to know.

"All the facts are beginning to tie in to my theory about why Rob Ladd has suddenly become a cheerleader." David held up his hand. "Now I know you don't want to talk about it, Olivia. But sometimes it helps if I think out loud. So I'll do all the talking and you can listen or not, it's up to you."

Grinning so that his dimple flashed, David glanced at Olivia. "But I'll bet you can't keep from listening."

Olivia crossed her arms and leaned back in the seat, her eyes closed.

"All right," David went on, watching the road again, "here we go. The Duffy Theory: One — For no reason that makes sense, Robinson Ladd

241

is made a cheerleader on the Tarenton High Varsity Squad. Two — A certain inquiring reporter, who shall remain nameless, tries to find out why. But when he does, he's kept out of squad practice, thrown out of a politician's office, and shut out by his girl friend, who's also on the squad."

Olivia's eyes flew open, but she didn't say anything.

"Now then," David continued. "Here comes the excting part. Three — This nameless, enterprising young reporter believes that Judson Abbott forced the coach to put Rob on the squad, which means that he's got something on her. But what? Does Ardith Engborg have a skeleton in her closet? A murky past?"

"Oh, don't be ridiculous," Olivia burst out.

"Ah ha! You *are* listening." They were at a stop light, and David turned around, grabbed his Sherlock Holmes hat off the back seat, and put it on. "It helps me think better," he explained.

He thought silently for a moment, and then sighed. "The trouble is, not even this hat can help me figure out what kind of ax Abbott could be holding over Mrs. Engborg's head. But I will. And when I do, then I'll blow the story wide open."

And the squad wide apart, Olivia thought. He's close, she told herself, feeling suddenly scared. He's really close to figuring it out. *Now* what was she going to do?

"Well, what do you think?" David asked.

242

"You know what I think," Olivia told him, managing to keep her voice cool in spite of the panic she felt. "I think you should just drop it."

David suddenly pulled the car over to the curb and shut the engine off. "I know you do, Olivia," he said. His cheerful mood had changed, and he spoke seriously. His blue eyes were as beautiful as ever, Olivia noticed, but they had a sad, lost look in them that she'd never seen before.

"But I can't do it," he said softly. "I just can't drop the story. I think it's important. And I know you think so, too. But for some reason, you're letting it come between us."

Olivia's throat suddenly had a lump in it about the size of a MacIntosh apple. It was too big to swallow, and much too big to talk through.

"I wish I knew why," David said. "If I did, then I could do something about it. But for now, all I can tell you is what I said before: I'm not giving up on us. But I'm not giving up on the story, either. So I guess you'll have to decide what you want."

I want this never to have happened, Olivia thought.

"When you decide, let me know, okay, Livvy?"

"Okay," Olivia whispered around the lump in her throat. Suddenly, she couldn't stay in the car any longer. She had to get out and get away from that look in David's eyes.

"I . . . think I'll walk the rest of the way home," she said. "It's not far, and I could use the fresh air."

Nodding, David leaned across her and pushed open her door. When he drew his hand back, he touched Olivia's shoulder, kissed her quickly on the cheek, and then started the car.

After David drove away, Olivia walked two blocks without seeing a thing. The tears were coming so fast and heavy that everything was one big blur, so when she finally stopped to search her pockets for a tissue, she wasn't really sure where she was.

Finally, though, her eyes cleared enough for her to look around, and when she saw that she was standing right in front of Tarenton High School, she almost smiled. At least she hadn't been walking around in a circle; her home was just a few more blocks away. If she could get in without her mother spotting her red, puffy eyes, then she could shut herself in her room and hibernate, at least until dinner.

It was colder now, and starting to get dark. Walking quickly, Olivia passed the high school and turned the corner. But when she saw Mrs. Engborg's blue hatchback in the parking lot, she stopped again.

The coach must be in her office, working on some cheers or something, Olivia thought. She changed directions and picked her way through the snow toward the side door of the school. You've got to let her know, she told herself. You've got to tell her how close David is to the truth. *Then* you can go home and cry some more.

* * *

Looking up from her desk, Mrs. Engborg's expression changed from annoyance to concern. Olivia Evans looked awful. Her eyes were puffy, her hair was blown and tangled, her boots were covered with snow, and she looked scared.

"Olivia!" The coach got up quickly and came around the desk. "What happened to you? Are you all right?"

Sinking into a chair, Olivia blew her nose and nodded. "Nothing happened," she said. "I know I look awful, but I'm really all right."

"*Something* must have happened," Mrs. Engborg insisted. "I'm glad you're not hurt, but would you mind telling me what you're doing here and why you look like you just saw a ghost?"

Olivia blew her nose again and took a shaky breath. "It's David Duffy," she said, and her eyes filled with tears again.

Mrs. Engborg put a hand on her shoulder. "Is there a problem between you?" she asked gently. Normally, she stayed strictly out of her cheerleaders' personal lives, unless it affected their work. But Olivia looked so completely bedraggled that she couldn't help asking.

"Yes," Olivia admitted, "but that's not why I'm here." She wiped her eyes and sat up straighter, determined to get control of herself. Falling apart wasn't going to help anything. "David's almost figured it out, Mrs. Engborg," she said. "I should have known he would. He said he's positive that Judson Abbott forced you to put Rob on the squad."

245

"I suppose I should have known he'd put two and two together," the coach admitted. "But he doesn't know why?"

"No. He thinks it's about you. That maybe you have some secret in your past that Mr. Abbott found out about."

Ardith Engborg laughed. "There's a lot in my past that I'd prefer no one knew about, but absolutely nothing I could be blackmailed with. David has quite an imagination."

"I know," Olivia agreed. "But he knows how to use that imagination. He's going to realize that you don't have any secrets, and then he's going to dream up some other theories. And one of them's going to be right."

"Maybe. Maybe not." The coach was worried, too, but she needed time to think, and she didn't want Olivia upset any more than she already was. "Now," she said briskly, "it's getting late. I'm glad you told me, Olivia, but there's no sense in two of us wringing our hands over this. There may be nothing I can do, anyway, so I want you to go home and relax."

Olivia stood up. "All right. I'm sorry I burst in here like that. I overreacted, I guess."

"Don't worry about it," the coach told her. She was already back at her desk, studying the papers on it. "And don't worry about anything else. That's an impossible order, I suppose," she said with a smile. "But try. Don't lose sleep over it, either. We have practice tomorrow at nine-thirty sharp."

When Olivia left the high school, she was calm on the outside. Her eyes were dry and her walk was quick and sure. But on the inside, she was still frightened. She'd go home all right, but she wouldn't relax.

She was worried about the squad, of course, but as she headed home through the dark evening, she was much more worried about David. Did they still have a chance? Or had she ruined things between them?

CHAPTER

22

"Do you know how I feel?" Jessica asked Patrick, her green eyes glowing. "I feel like I could run a marathon, or do the longest ski jump on record, or — "

"How about jumping into the deep end of a swimming pool?" Patrick suggested.

Leaning over, Jessica kissed him on the cheek. "I already did that," she said.

They were in Patrick's moving van, on the way to Tarenton High. Patrick had a job to do, but he couldn't wait until that afternoon to see Jessica, so he'd picked her up at eight-fifteen in the morning. The day was cold but bright, and the snow sparkled like crystal in the sun.

"I just have so much energy," Jessica said, as they pulled up to the school. "I never knew falling in love would make me want to dance and run and jump up and down."

Patrick laughed and put his arm around her. "Well, it's a good thing you have practice now, I guess. You can work off some of that energy." Kissing her softly, he added, "But save some for me, okay?"

"Don't worry," Jessica told him with a grin. "There'll be plenty left over. See you later!"

Still grinning, Jessica got out of the van and ran across the parking lot. She was early for practice, but she couldn't have walked if she'd been ordered to. She felt too good, too incredibly happy to do anything but run.

Just as she reached the door, Sean's red car zipped into the lot, with Tara in the passenger seat. Jessica waited while they came over to her. "What are you guys doing here so early?" she asked.

"We just had an enormous breakfast at the Pancake House," Tara explained. "We were celebrating."

"Celebrating what?"

"Oh, just the fact that we're on the same side again," Sean said, winking at Tara.

"Anyway," Tara laughed, "we ate too much. And we decided to come here and work it off instead of sitting in the Pancake House for another half hour and letting all that syrup and butter become a permanent part of our bodies."

"What brings *you* here ahead of schedule?" Sean asked Jessica as they went inside.

"Patrick," Jessica replied. "He had a job and he dropped me off early. But I'm ready to work out, too. I feel like I could do back walkovers forever."

Before they reached the gym, the outside door opened, and Peter and Hope walked in, holding hands and laughing.

"What's *your* reason?" Sean called to them.

"Reason for what?" Peter asked.

"For getting here early. Jessica's in love and Tara and I are stuffed," Sean explained. "What brings you two to practice forty minutes ahead of time?"

"Are we that early?" Hope asked.

"We took a drive," Peter said to the others. "I guess neither one of us was paying any attention to the time."

"Two more in love," Tara remarked. "Well, since we're here, we might as well get started."

"Sure," Jessica said. "Why not? We don't need to wait for Olivia to warm up."

"And we sure don't need to wait for Ladd," Sean added, his eyes gleaming.

In high spirits, the five cheerleaders went into the gym. Sean turned on the lights, Tara turned on the transistor radio she'd brought, and still laughing, they began to warm up.

Down the hall, Ardith Engborg sat in her office, thinking about what Olivia had told her the day before. She'd thought about it until she went to sleep that night and when she woke up in the morning, it was still on her mind. Troubled and restless, the coach had come to the high school early, hoping that in her office, catching up on some paperwork, she'd be able to put it out of her mind.

It wasn't working. Ardith Engborg, in spite of what she'd said to Olivia, was worried. If David Duffy, using his imagination or his reporter's nose, or both, had discovered the reason Rob Ladd was on the squad, then Judson Abbott was going to make things extremely difficult. David didn't even have to get it right, Ardith thought. All he had to do was write a column outlining his suspicions, and the damage would be done.

Ardith Engborg loathed being in a bind, and she rarely got into one. But when she did, she always got out. This bind, though, was different. It had been tight from the beginning, and it was getting even tighter.

There has to be a way out, Ardith thought. Just keep looking, and you'll find it. You always have.

With a determined nod, Ardith went back to her paperwork, telling herself to shut out everything else for the moment.

It would have worked except for the music. She kept hearing music — not very loud, but loud enough to distract her. Lifting her head, she listened closely. It seemed to be coming from the gym. Still twenty minutes to practice, she thought, but maybe one of the cheerleaders came in early.

Then the coach heard a shout of laughter, genuine laughter. She hadn't heard that sound since she'd put Rob on the squad. Curious, she left her office and went down the hall to investigate.

Inside the gym, the five cheerleaders had warmed up quickly. Still feeling like they could fly, they decided to go through some "old" moves — the kinds of moves that had made the squad famous.

They hadn't really discussed it at all. But after they'd warmed up and were sitting around joking, Sean suddenly jumped to his feet. He stood poised for a moment, then took off in a series of front flips that brought him clear across the gym.

Wordlessly, Peter joined him, and then Jessica did. After exchanging grins, Tara and Hope leaped up and began doing cartwheels and splits.

Then, as if they could read each other's minds, the five of them stopped and got into position for a cheer. Tara and Hope kept up an intricate dance step, waving their pompons in a pattern of flashing color. Peter and Sean did simultaneous stag leaps, followed by back flips. Then Jessica, her long legs pushing her high into the air, bounded across the gym and onto Sean's shoulders. They did the routine in complete silence, but they did it with smiles on their faces.

"Wow!" Sean said, lifting Jessica down. "That felt fantastic!"

"I'll bet it looked great, too," Peter agreed. "Except for one thing."

"What?"

"I'm missing my partner," Peter said, pointing

252

to his empty shoulders where Olivia would have been. "I demand a redo, and this time, *I* get to catch Jessica."

They all burst out laughing, and that was the laughter Ardith Engborg had heard. Now, as the coach peered around the gym doors, she saw the five cheerleaders begin the routine again, still without chanting the words.

It's almost like a dance, she thought. A beautiful dance. And it didn't need words. The expressions on the cheerleaders' faces said it all: Joyful and exuberant, completely in tune with each other, they were loving every minute of it.

Stepping back into the hall, Mrs. Engborg felt completely torn. This was the kind of squad she'd worked so hard for over the years, and she didn't want to let it go. It would have to be taken away from her.

Which is exactly what will happen, she thought, if you remove Robinson Ladd from the squad. But don't those cheerleaders deserve some say in this? After all, it's their squad as much as yours. Maybe they'd rather keep it together, even with Rob, than let it go. At least talk to them first.

As she walked back to her office, she made up her mind. She'd talk to the cheerleaders and ask them what they thought. If they were willing to risk what would happen if the truth about Rob Ladd's presence on the squad were known, then when the principal, Mrs. Oetjen, got back from vacation, Ardith would tell everything.

If the whole thing were made public, Judson

Abbott would find a way to get back at her, she knew that. It might take him a while, but he'd make good on his promise to cut funding for cheerleading. But if the Tarenton High Varsity Squad had to go, then it deserved to go out being the best it could be. It deserved to go out on top.

Talk to the cheerleaders, she told herself. Find out if they're willing to take the risk. Reaching her office, Mrs. Engborg had to admit that she still wasn't sure what she wanted to happen — to keep going at any cost, or to risk losing the varsity squad.

Fifteen minutes later, when Ardith Engborg strode into the gym, seven cheerleaders were there. A very droopy-mouthed, sad-eyed Olivia, and a calm, composed Rob Ladd had joined the other five.

At first, Mrs. Engborg was tempted to have the entire discussion in front of Rob. But now she decided against it. True, he'd played a dirty game, and he deserved to be humiliated. But she didn't want to be the one to do it. She'd call a special meeting later in the day and talk to the other six then.

"All right," she said to the group. "We missed yesterday because of the storm, so I expect you to work extra hard today. The new year's coming, and after that, Garrison High is coming. Let's be ready for them."

Olivia raised her hand. "Mrs. Engborg, I was

late. I'm sorry, but I didn't get a chance to warm up. May I take five minutes?"

"All right, Olivia," Mrs. Engborg said sharply. Then she looked more closely at the girl's tired face. Olivia's been through the wringer with me on this, she thought. "Go ahead," she told the captain, her voice softening.

Nodding her thanks, Olivia dragged herself up off the floor and bent to touch her toes. They seemed much harder to reach than usual, so she straightened up and tried some leg stretches. Pretending she was a fencer, she lunged to one side and then the other. Her legs felt like lead.

"Olivia?" Hope asked. "Are you okay?"

"Don't ask her that," Tara said with a laugh. "She'll accuse you of acting like her mother. But really, Olivia," she went on, "you look kind of upset or something."

Flopping onto the floor, Olivia shook her head. "I'm okay," she told them. "I just didn't sleep too well." That's the understatement of the year, she thought. You slept exactly two hours.

Not wanting to bother her, Hope drifted off to be with Peter, but Tara stayed. "Olivia," she said after minute, "could I tell you something?"

"I'm supposed to be warming up," Olivia said. Then she saw that the coach was bent over her notepad, not paying any attention. "But since I can barely move, go ahead."

Tara hesitated. She wasn't used to apologizing, but she felt she had to. "I just wanted you to know that you were right about the way I was acting. You know, with Sean and Rob."

Olivia looked at her, surprised, and Tara blushed. "I didn't mean to do it," she went on. "And I'm sorry. I told Sean so, too."

"That's great, Tara." Olivia meant it; she was glad that some things were turning out right, at least.

Relieved that the apology was out of the way, Tara brightened up. "Listen," she said eagerly, "You'll never guess what Rob told me. He wants Sean off the squad."

That made Olivia forget all her problems for the moment. "He *what*? He said that to you?"

"He said he doesn't think Sean fits in," Tara told her. "And I'm pretty sure he plans to keep digging at Sean until he quits."

"Well, I've noticed that Sean hasn't been acting too happy lately," Olivia said. "I always thought it was impossible, but he's actually been down on himself. Maybe Rob's plan is working."

"It was, until I talked to Sean." Tara said. Laughing, she told Olivia what had happened in the billiard room at the Ladd house. "I told him to straighten up and fly right. And he's going to do it. So we don't have to worry about that."

"Good." Olivia's eyes brightened, knowing that Sean was on to Rob now, and ready for him. Then she looked at Rob, who was sitting by himself. Now not even Tara was interested in him, she thought. If he'd been a different person,

Olivia might have felt sorry for him. There was nothing worse than being isolated, shut out by your own teammates.

But Rob, as usual, looked as if nothing was bothering him. He's so sure of himself, Olivia thought. He's got us over a barrel, and he's got nothing to worry about. We're the ones in trouble. Her spirits took a dive again. "I'm glad you talked some sense into Sean, Tara," she said listlessly. "But if Sean had quit, I wouldn't have blamed him. I'm not even sure how much longer *I* can hang on."

Tara's eyes widened. "You? But, Olivia, you're the captain. You *can't* quit."

"It's just like Sean said the other day," Olivia told her. "It's no fun. Why bother going through all the moves and stuff if we can't enjoy it?"

Jessica, who'd been sitting nearby in a happy daze, barely listening, suddenly straightened up. "Is this our captain speaking?" she said, trying to joke Olivia to her senses. "I can't believe what I just heard."

"Want me to say it again?" Olivia asked. "Okay, I will. The squad stinks, and I don't enjoy being on it."

Jessica's smile disappeared. "Listen, Olivia, I know how you feel. But the rest of us got here early, and you know what we did? We did one of our old routines, and it felt great."

"It really did," Tara agreed. "I wish you'd been here."

"Maybe . . . I don't know," Jessica said, "maybe we can get together sometime — just the six of us — and practice. It might help."

"Help what?" Olivia asked skeptically. "We'll be the best squad in the state, but nobody'll see us. Because when we perform, there'll be seven of us. and then we'll be the worst."

Exchanging glances, Tara and Jessica left Olivia alone to finish her warm-ups.

"I guess she's not in the mood to see the bright side of things," Tara remarked.

"She's right in a way, though," Jessica said. "I mean, working out on our own is nice. But nobody's going to clap, nobody's going to shout and stamp their feet. I see what Olivia means. We're performers, and performers need an audience."

Before Tara could think of something to say to that, Mrs. Engborg clapped her hands.

"Okay," she said. "Positions for 'Let's Move.' "

The cheerleaders took their places quickly, except for Olivia, who looked like she was wading through water.

> "Let's move!
> Let's go!
> Let's really show. . . ."

"Stop," Ardith called. "Some of you are distinctly lacking in what I call 'oomph,' " she said. She tried not to look at Olivia, but it was Olivia she was talking about. That worried her. Of all the cheerleaders, Mrs. Engborg expected Olivia

258

Evans to be the one to carry the squad's banner and say, Yes, let's dump Rob and take our chances! But now she looked like the squad, good or bad, meant nothing to her.

Frowning, the coach said, "Start again, please. With oomph this time."

> "Let's move!
> Let's go. . . ."

"Stop!" Mrs. Engborg called again. But this time, she wasn't looking at the cheerleaders. She was looking at Judson Abbott, who was standing in the doorway.

Smiling, Abbott stepped inside, holding up his hands. "I know, I know," he said smoothly, "practices are closed. But I thought you might make an exception, just this once."

"No exceptions," Ardith said coolly.

Moving aside, Judson Abbott gestured to a tall, slender man who had been standing behind him.

Still smiling his confident smile, Abbott asked, "Not even for a senator?"

CHAPTER

23

"Oh, brother!" Sean whispered to Tara. "What's he doing here? We can't vote."

Tara giggled. "No, but our parents can. He's probably hoping we'll say good things about him at home." She glanced at the Senator, who was conferring with Judson Abbott and Ardith Engborg. "Funny," she remarked. "He doesn't look like the kind of man who'd have a son like Rob. He actually looks like a nice, decent person."

It was true. Rob was tall and slender, and so was his father, but the resemblance stopped there. Senator William Ladd had a wide-open, friendly face, thick dark hair, and a lively smile.

"Yeah, he looks okay," Sean admitted. "But remember, he's a politician. And he *is* Rob's father. Somebody had to make Rob the way he is, he couldn't have been born that way."

"Born?" Tara whispered, laughing again. "According to you, he crawled out from under a rock, remember?"

Rob had gone over to talk to his father, too, and as the other cheerleaders watched, they saw Ardith shake her head. "I'm sorry," they heard her say. "You've put me in an awkward position, and I don't want to seem rude, but I'm afraid I have to insist on closed practices."

"Way to go, coach," Peter said under his breath.

Judson Abbott started to argue, but Senator Ladd shot him a quick look and smiled pleasantly. "I can't say I'm not disappointed," he told the coach. "After all, I've heard great things about your cheerleaders. They have quite an impressive reputation."

Mrs. Engborg nodded.

"And since I'm so rarely at home," the Senator went on, "I was hoping I could catch a quick glimpse of them today. But you're the coach, Mrs. Engborg. Judd," he said, turning to Abbott, "let's go so they can work."

"Excuse me. Mrs. Engborg?" Sean jumped up and walked halfway to the group at the door. "I don't mean to interfere, but something the Senator said got me to thinking."

"What is it, Sean?" the coach asked, looking slightly annoyed.

"Well, Senator Ladd said that he isn't home very often and he won't get many chances to see Rob on the squad." Sean sounded as if the whole

261

situation made him very sad. "My father's a busy man, too, and he almost never gets to see me cheer. It sure would mean a lot to me if he could."

Mrs. Engborg shifted impatiently. "What's your point, Sean?"

"I was just thinking that it must mean a lot to Rob, too, to have his father see him perform," Sean explained. "And since Senator Ladd is already here, why not let him watch for just a little while? Then you can close the practice again. I sure wouldn't mind." Turning to the other cheerleaders, he asked, "How about you guys? Would you mind?"

Sean's dark eyes were sparkling wickedly, and his mouth was curved in a mischievous smile, but only the cheerleaders saw him. And only the cheerleaders knew what he was up to. Let's let Rob's daddy see just how bad his son is, Sean was silently saying. Even if he doesn't care, even if he's the one who got Rob on the squad, it'll have to drive him crazy, seeing his little boy making a jerk out of himself. So come on, let's do it — let's drive him crazy. We'll all feel a lot better.

The five cheerleaders looked at Rob, then they looked at each other. One by one, they returned his grin. "No, we don't mind," Tara said, speaking for the rest of them. "Of course, if you're really against it, Mrs. Engborg, then. . . . Well, you're the coach. But how many times do we get to give a private performance for a senator?"

When Tara wanted to, she could really pour

on the charm, and this time, she had it up full blast. If it had been just Mrs. Engborg, of course, she would have been wasting her time. The coach was immune to charm.

But maybe the coach wasn't immune to the combination of her cheerleaders, plus a senator, plus Judson Abbott. Or maybe she had an inkling of what Sean was trying to do, and decided to go along with it. No one could tell what she was thinking from the expression on her face, but after looking sharply at the cheerleaders, she finally nodded.

"All right," she said. "I suppose it won't do any harm. But just until we take a break," she added. "Then I'll want the gym cleared again."

"You have my word, Mrs. Engborg." Senator Ladd said. He clapped Rob on the shoulder, and then walked toward the bleachers, followed by a smug-looking Judson Abbott.

Rob joined the rest of the squad, and the seven cheerleaders got in position.

"Remember," Sean whispered to Peter, "lot's of oomph."

"It's a little hard to put oomph into this cheer," Peter whispered back.

"Use your imagination," Sean told him. "Pretend that if you don't do it right, Hope'll never speak to you again."

Peter laughed out loud, which earned him a frown from the coach.

"Let's get to work," she called. "Let's move."

"Let's move!
Let's go!
Let's really show. . . ."

At first, it seemed like Sean's plan to humiliate Rob was going to fall flat on its face. The first half of the cheer went flawlessly. Hands were clapped, feet were stamped in time and in unison. Smiles were in place, voices were loud and clear, as if there were five hundred people in the bleachers watching the final few seconds of a tie ball game.

"Who's best,
Who's tops. . . ."

For the first time since they'd done this cheer, Sean deliberately tried to get his pompon to tangle with Rob's. He leaned a little farther to the left than he had to, stretching his arm until it almost hurt. But no luck. They got through the pompon swinging without a collision. Now he had to pin his hopes on the straddle jump.

"Who's number one,
Tarenton!"

Finally, Rob's lack of talent showed through. As usual, his straddle jump wasn't anywhere near as high as the other two guys'. His toes pointed up instead of out, and his arms and fingers weren't extended the way they should have been.

But it wasn't enough, Sean thought. Anyone could goof. How was the senator to know that this was the *best* his son could do? In fact, nine times out of ten, it was probably *better* than he could do.

Mrs. Engborg had them go through it one more time, and then she said, "That's enough on that one for the moment. There's still plenty of room for improvement, especially on the end. But I don't want to work it into the ground, so we'll come back to it later."

Rob, whose second jump hadn't been quite as good as his first — which made it way below average — glanced over at Sean and raised an eyebrow. Sean ignored him.

"Let's work on 'You're the Best' now," Mrs. Engborg said. "We've been away from it for a while. and since Tarenton usually beats Garrison, we should have it prepared. Positions. please."

Now it was Sean who looked at Rob. And what he saw made him chuckle to himself. Rob hadn't been expecting another cheer. and it was obvious he didn't like the idea at all. He'd done one fairly well, but he'd been lucky. He knew it, and Sean knew it. But now what? What was going to happen when he had to go through a routine he hadn't practiced in four or five days?

You're on your own, Robinson, Sean thought. How do you like it?

"Let's go," Mrs. Engborg called.

> "You're the best,
> Don't let it slide,
> Tell that team,
> To step aside!"

"Hold it," Mrs. Engborg said. "You're way out of step. Let's walk through it until we get it right."

Walking through a cheer was one of the dullest things in the world, about as exciting as standing in line at the supermarket. But Senator Ladd seemed fascinated, Sean noticed. He was beginning to wish the man would go away. Anybody who knew cheerleading would know that Rob didn't belong on the squad, but the Senator knew politics, not cheerleading.

Slowly, they walked through the cheer. It had been simple enough to begin with, and now that the boys weren't doing stag leaps at the end, it looked like something a dance teacher would give a bunch of first-graders to do. Finally they reached the end, boys with their hands on their hips, girls doing the splits.

Mrs. Engborg stared at them for a minute, thinking. "You were right," she admitted, looking at Jessica and Peter. "It *is* off-balance now. The girls leap first before they land in the splits, and with the boys not doing stag leaps anymore, it's flat."

266

"We could just slide into the splits," Hope suggested. "We don't have to leap first."

"That might help," the coach agreed. "But that'll take just about all the punch out of it." She thought some more. "Okay, try this: On the word *step*, I want everyone to give a fast, tight spin in place. Then on *aside,* you'll be out of the spin — boys standing, girls sliding into the splits. Got it?"

Everyone nodded, and got ready. Sean noticed that the Senator was leaning forward, a frown on his face. He bent over and said something to Abbott, who shrugged and said something back. But the Senator's frown didn't disappear.

"Let's go," the coach called.

Everyone got it right the first time, except Rob, whose spin was wide and sloppy.

"Again," said the coach.

They did it again and again and again. Then they started the cheer from the top. The coach stopped them halfway through. "Okay, let's take a break," she said. "We'll pick it up again where we left off, in fifteen minutes." Turning to the Senator and Abbott, she said, "I think that gives you an idea of what we go through."

Not a very good idea, Sean said to himself. We're usually beat by break time, and I haven't even worked up a sweat.

The Senator was making his way down from the stands, looking very thoughtful. "Thank you, Mrs. Engborg," he said when he reached the

267

floor. "I appreciate your letting me watch. I enjoyed it."

"You're welcome."

"I was under the impression, though," he went on, "that this varsity squad was famous for its tough, high-flying routines. I guess I'm a little disappointed that I didn't get to see any of that."

You *won't* see any of that, either, Sean thought. Not as long as your son's here.

Mrs. Engborg gave a very diplomatic answer. "This cheer *is* one of our easiest," she admitted. "But as I said, we use it a lot when the Tarenton team is ahead. And since we'll be playing Garrison, the odds are that we'll win, so I like to be prepared."

Still looking thoughtful, the Senator nodded. "I see. Well, thank you again. Now, I hope you don't mind, but I'd like to speak to Rob out in the hall for a few minutes."

"That's fine, as long as he's back when the break's over."

The Senator didn't answer. He'd gestured for Rob to follow, and was already halfway to the door.

Mrs. Engborg went down the hall to her office, and with Rob, the Senator, and Abbott out of the gym, the cheerleaders relaxed.

"Hey, this is like old times, huh?" Sean said. "Just the six of us."

"I loved the way you sounded so sincere about letting the senator watch," Tara told him.

"What do you mean, 'sounded'?" Sean asked with a grin. "I *was* sincere. "I really wanted the guy to see his son in action."

"You wanted to put Rob on the spot, too," Peter said. "Admit it."

"Sure I did," Sean said. "Unfortunately, I don't think it worked." ¡

"I don't know," Jessica commented. "Rob looked awfully uncomfortable to me. I got the feeling he didn't like his father watching."

"I got that feeling, too," Hope agreed. "I guess it isn't very nice, wanting someone to be embarrassed, but I couldn't help wishing Rob would look really bad."

"Don't apologize," Sean said. "I was hoping he'd fall flat on his face. But I guess he's saving that for the first game."

Everyone laughed, except Olivia, who was lying on her back, staring at the ceiling. The others noticed that she hadn't joined in their joking, which wasn't like her at all. Tara and Jessica knew she was upset, but it was obvious that she wanted to be left alone, so they didn't bother her.

Except for Olivia's moodiness, it did seem like old times. Waiting for the break to be over, the cheerleaders sat around, sipping water or juice, and talked quietly together about their holidays, about the storm, about what they were going to do for New Year's Eve.

"Is anybody planning a party?" Peter asked.

Everyone looked at Sean.

"Not me," he said. "I haven't recovered from the one I gave at Christmas yet. It was a real flop."

"Yeah, everyone was mad at everyone else," Peter agreed, smiling at Hope.

"Nobody's mad now, though," Tara said. "Why don't I talk to my parents? I'm sure they'll let me have a party. If they do, you're all invited."

"What about you-know-who?" Sean asked, glancing at the doorway.

Tara started to answer, but before she could, they heard the Senator's voice. It was loud, and it was angry.

"I'm absolutely appalled," he said. "If I'd had any idea at all — "

"Ah, Senator," Judson Abbott broke in. "I can explain — "

The Senator cut him off. "I don't want to hear it. You know what I want, and I want it done now!" He said something more, but now he was speaking quietly, and the cheerleaders weren't able to hear.

"I wonder what that's all about," Peter said.

"Politics, probably," Sean remarked. "Want me to hide behind the door and listen?"

"No, don't," Tara told him. "They'll see you."

"No, they won't," Sean assured her. "I'll be very, very sneaky." Getting to his feet, he raced silently across the gym and hid himself behind the door. He listened for a moment, and then called out, "Too late. They've gone down the hall."

"Come on over here," Tara said. "You look ridiculous crouched behind that door."

"Wait a minute." Sean held out his hand. "They're coming back." He waited again, ready to eavesdrop, but it was too late. Accompanied by Mrs. Engborg, the Senator, Rob, and Judson Abbott walked into the gym. Trying to look casual, Sean strolled back to the other cheerleaders.

The Senator cleared his throat. "I have to be going now," he said to the six of them, "but I just wanted to say thanks for letting me watch. I've heard great things about your squad, and I know you work hard to be the best. So keep on working, and don't let anybody stop you." Clearing his throat again, he looked at Rob. "Now, my son has something to say to you, so I'll leave him to it."

Rob nodded to his father, and then the Senator and Abbott left the gym.

All eyes were on Rob. He stared back at each of them, looking longest at Sean, and then his mouth curved into that half smile that they'd all come to dislike so much.

"This won't take long," he said. "I'm quitting the squad." He paused, as if he expected someone to say something, but no one did. No one could.

Rob looked at Mrs. Engborg, then back at the cheerleaders. Then he sauntered over to the corner and picked up his canvas bag. Slinging it over his shoulder, he crossed to the door and stopped, his hand on the bar.

Turning, still, smiling, he said, "Well, so long. I can't say it's been fun, but I will say it's been interesting."

With that, Robinson Ladd walked out the door.

CHAPTER

Shocked silence greeted Rob's departure. Everyone stared at the door, wondering if it had all been a bad joke. None of them would have put it past Rob to suddenly reappear and say, "Gotcha!"

But after a full minute of silence, it became obvious that Rob wasn't going to come back. He was off the squad, out of the gym, and out of their lives.

In a small voice, as if she still couldn't quite believe it, Hope asked, "Did what I think just happened happen?"

Peter nodded. "I think so," he said, speaking just as quietly. "I think he really quit."

"You're not dreaming," Mrs. Engborg told them dryly, a grin tugging at her lips. "It's real. Rob quit the squad."

"Well? What are we waiting for?" Sean asked. Leaping exuberantly to his feet, his eyes sparkling, he let out a whoop of delight. Then, as if he couldn't hold himself back, he took a running jump and executed a perfect forward flip, laughing and shouting the whole time.

His action was contagious, and suddenly there were six cheerleaders doing cartwheels and flips, giggling crazily with relief. They stopped long enough to form a circle, hugging each other and jumping up and down; then they broke apart and bounded across the gym again.

Mrs. Engborg stood and watched them, smiling, until slowly they began to wind down. First Peter, then Hope and Tara, then Olivia, Jessica, and finally Sean flung themselves onto the floor, panting, gasping, and still laughing.

Jessica was the first to recover. "Mrs. Engborg," she said, "what happened? How did you get Rob to quit?"

"I didn't," the coach replied. "His father did."

"But why?" Hope asked. "Didn't he want him to be on it?"

"I'm sure he did, as long as Rob earned the right to be on it," Mrs. Engborg said. "But once he found out about Rob's and Abbott's methods, he insisted that he remove himself."

"How'd he find out?" Sean asked. "Did you tell him?"

Mrs. Engborg shook her head and laughed. "No, he figured it out by himself. You heard what he said — he's aware of this squad's reputation. And when he saw that it wasn't living up to that reputation. he wanted to know why."

"And you told him the whole story?"

"No, I guess Rob and Judson Abbott did," the coach said. "I was in my office when they had their discussion, so I'm not sure who said what. I couldn't help overhearing a few things. though," she admitted. "First the Senator asked Rob why the stag leaps had been cut."

"Yeah?" Sean looked pleased. "What did Rob say?"

"He said they were too difficult."

"Ha. Too difficult for *him*, he meant."

"Evidently, the Senator had his suspicions," Mrs. Engborg said, "because he asked Rob out right what he meant by that. He said as far as he knew. this squad could do just about anything. And then he asked Rob if he was the one who couldn't do the stag leap."

"All right!" Sean slapped his thigh in satisfaction.

"What did Rob say to that?" Tara asked.

"I don't know," the coach told her. "That's when I closed my door. The next thing I knew, the three of them were in my office. First the Senator apologized. then Rob and Judson Abbott did. Rob was supposed to apologize to the squad, too," she said, "but as you saw, he didn't bother."

"Of course he didn't," Jessica commented. "He wasn't sorry."

"I guess you're right, Jessica," Hope said. "I keep trying to feel bad for him, but I can't."

275

"Don't blame yourself for feeling that way," Olivia told her. "It's hard to feel bad for somebody like Rob. He didn't even have the decency to look embarrassed. I don't think this entire thing touched him at all."

"You may be right, Olivia," Mrs. Engborg said. "Rob doesn't seem to have much of a conscience. But I do, and since he didn't apologize, I will."

Everyone started to talk, to tell her she didn't have anything to be sorry for, but the coach held up her hand. "Thank you, but you're wrong. I got you into this and I shouldn't have. I finally realized it this morning. And I was going to call a meeting later, without Rob, to ask you what you wanted to do. Whether you wanted to go on with Rob, or to have me remove him from the squad and see what happened."

Ardith Engborg took a deep breath. "As I said, I decided to do that this morning. But I should have decided it a long time ago, and for that, I apologize." Another deep breath, a smile, and with a clap of her hands, the coach was back to normal. "Now, the break's over. Let's get to work!"

Still buzzing with excitement, their bodies filled with energy, the six cheerleaders scrambled to their feet and got in position for "You're the Best."

They *are* the best, Mrs. Engborg thought, watching them. And now, they have a chance to stay that way.

"Oh, wait," Sean said, his cocky smile back in place. "Mrs. Engborg, I take it we're putting the stag leaps in again, right?"

"Right," the coach replied. "And don't forget the oomph."

She didn't need to tell them that. With Rob gone, the cheerleaders had enough oomph to fill the gym twice over.

"Could you believe it?" Tara asked in the girls' locker room after practice. "We were so good in there after Rob left! He's gone and it feels like he was never even here!"

"I know what you mean," Jessica said. "I wish we'd worked on a harder cheer. I've got too much energy left over." Then, remembering what Patrick had said about saving some of that energy for him, she smiled. Maybe it was a good thing the cheer hadn't been hard, after all.

"I guess Rob didn't do any damage," Hope said. "We thought he was ruining us, but I think we're better than ever."

"I feel great!" Tara shouted, pulling on a giant turquoise and yellow sweat shirt that almost reached her knees. "I feel hungry, too. Who's ready for pizza?"

"I am," Jessica said immediately. "Patrick's picking me up, so we'll meet you at the Pizza Palace."

"So will Peter and I." Hope stepped into some soft blue corduroy pants and laughed. "I guess I should ask him first, but I'm sure he's starving."

"Good. Let's order one with the works," Tara said, laughing. "After all, we're celebrating." Turning to Olivia, she asked, "Why don't you ride with Sean and me?"

Olivia, brushing her hair, smiled, but shook her head. "I don't think so," she said. "You guys go on, okay? I'll be there in a little while."

"Okay," Tara said. "But don't be too long. We don't want to start the celebration without you, and we're famished!"

Olivia kept her smile on until the three other cheerleaders left the locker room. Then, frowning, she sat down on one of the benches and stared at her feet.

Olivia was as glad as anyone that Rob was off the squad. When he quit, she'd felt just like the others — so happy, she couldn't sit still. It was going to be great now, the six of them working together like a team. They *were* a team, she thought, one of the best.

But now that some of the excitement had worn off, she couldn't help thinking about David. Hope said that Rob hadn't done any damage. But that wasn't quite true. He had done some damage — he'd hurt Olivia's relationship with David Duffy, and she wasn't sure if the damage could be repaired.

Walt was gone now, and Olivia realized she didn't care. She'd been using Walt as an excuse to avoid David and his questions. It had been so convenient, having Walt here. But it wasn't Walt she wanted. It was David Duffy, and she'd done everything she could to push him away.

Still studying her feet, Olivia discovered that there was a hole in her left sock. Go home and sew it up, she told herself. No, go to The Pizza Palace and celebrate with the others. They'll be disappointed if you don't, and maybe if you eat enough pizza, you'll forget about David.

Pulling on her boots and jacket, Olivia stood up and left the locker room. She didn't want to drag everyone down by moping over her pizza, but eating pizza was more fun than sewing up a hole in her sock. Besides, the others would probably still be too happy to notice that she was feeling rotten.

The hall was empty and dim, but as Olivia walked down it, the outer door opened, letting in enough light for her to see a tall boy wearing a Sherlock Holmes hat on his thick blond hair.

"Olivia!" David Duffy shouted. running toward her. "I just heard the news," he said excitedly. "What a story! Blackmail, no less! I knew something fishy was going on!"

"Yes. you did," Olivia agreed.

"It's the best story I've ever been on," David said. "I just wish I'd figured it out myself." He reached up and patted his Sherlock Holmes hat. "Of course, I didn't have this at the beginning. But the next time there's a cover-up, look out!"

"You must be really happy," Olivia commented.

"Sure I am," David said. "Aren't you?"

"Well, I'm glad it's all over," she told him. "It was awful having Rob on the squad."

"And what about covering it up?" David asked.

Olivia felt her throat tighten. "That was even worse," she said softly, wishing he hadn't mentioned it.

"It must have been tough," David agreed, "not being able to tell anyone about it."

Olivia nodded, keeping her eyes on the floor. Reaching his hand out, David lifted her chin and studied her face. "I see a lot of worry here," he said. "I really gave you a rough time, didn't I? Bugging you day after day to tell me about Rob Ladd when you'd promised not to say a word to anyone." Very gently, he stroked her cheek. "I'm so sorry, Olivia."

"Sorry?" Olivia wasn't sure she'd heard him right. "I thought you were mad at me."

"I was, a little," David admitted. "Especially after Walt got here. I kept telling myself that it was over between you two, but when you started spending every free minute with him — "

"It *is* over," Olivia told him firmly. "He was just a convenient escape, that's all."

David nodded. "An escape from me," he said. "I can understand that. All I wanted to talk about was Rob Ladd, and you couldn't tell me what was going on. Boy, I must have driven you crazy!"

Olivia laughed. It was dark in the hall, but in

her mind, the sun had just come out. "You're driving me crazy right now," she said.

"Sorry, I'll drop the subject of Rob Ladd. Forever." David promised.

"That's not what I meant." Olivia laughed again. "I mean you're driving me crazy by standing there, a foot away from me. I want you closer." she said softly. "I want to feel your arms around me."

"Ah ha!" David's blue eyes lit up happily. "That's an easy order to fill."

Without another word, they both took a step and wrapped their arms around each other. When they kissed, Olivia felt all the tension of the past two weeks disappear. By the second kiss, she'd forgotten it had ever existed.

Sighing, David moved his lips from her mouth to her eyes, and over to her ear. His breath tickled when he spoke. "What shall we do now?" he whispered.

Laughing, Olivia took his hand. "Now," she said, "we go celebrate."

Their arms around each other's waists, the two of them drifted down the hall and out into the clear, cold day. Hope had been right after all, Olivia thought happily. No damage had been done.

"Come on along,
We're going strong!"

Standing in a line, their hands on the shoulders of the person in front of them, the six cheerleaders of the Tarenton High Varsity Squad turned their heads toward the crowd in the stands. Their smiles were genuine, their voices jubilant. It was the first game of the new year, and Tarenton was ahead by twelve points.

"On your feet,
And shout along!"

With a roar, the fans leaped to their feet. Olivia, at the head of the "train," broke free and did a front walkover. Jessica, at the other end, did a back walkover. Tara and Hope leaped high, knees bent until their feet almost touched their arched backs, while behind them, Sean and Rob did perfect stag leaps.

Within seconds, the cheerleaders were back in line, their right arms whirling like wheels, while the crowd thundered in one voice:

"Tarenton's high,
Garrison's low,
Tarenton's hot,
Garrison's not!"

The cheerleaders went through the routine again, this time ending with Jessica and Olivia on the boys' shoulders, while the crowd roared its approval.

Olivia, glancing up in the stands, saw David shouting with the rest of the crowd, but his eyes were on her. She felt like blowing him a kiss, but the coach would definitely not approve of that. With her eyes, she tried to send him a message. David must have gotten it — cupping his hands, he mouthed the words, "Love you, too!"

"We're not wrong,
So shout along!"

Hope saw her family in the stands, looking proud, especially her mother. Catching Peter's eye, she smiled. Peter had seen them, too, and he knew they were cheering for him as much as they were for their daughter.

"Clap your hands,
We're going strong!"

Jessica didn't see Patrick; she was concentrating too hard. But she knew he was there for her, and she knew he always would be.

Tara, who always checked the stands, caught sight of a good-looking boy from her English class and sent him a smile that was so bright, and yet so intimate, that the boy nearly fell off the bleacher.

Sean didn't have anybody watching just him — neither a girl, nor his father. But tonight it didn't matter. His father would make it some time, and

283

Sean knew his love life wouldn't stay on hold forever. So tonight he jumped for the pure joy of it, and he jumped higher than he ever had in his life.

It was as if nothing had changed, as if Rob Ladd had never slithered his way across their path. The cheerleaders performed with all the energy, precision, grace, and split-second timing that had earned them their reputation for being the best in the tri-state region.

But that night, there was more to it. Something *had* changed. It wasn't anything anyone could see, or put their finger on. It was the oomph Mrs. Engborg was constantly urging them to show. That night it showed brighter than ever, because it didn't come from just their legs and arms and voices. That night, it came from their hearts.

When Sean gets involved with a girl from rival Garrison High, he discovers that she's out to steal more than just his heart. Read Cheerleaders #25, Stealing Secrets.